D0989229

When the itch for new ink takes over, NHL star Randy Ballistic commissions his trusted tattoo artist to design a new sleeve, and the rest of the PUCKED boys decide it's time to commemorate their love of hockey with a team tattoo.

But it can't just be about the boys—the PUCKED girls want in on the action, too. Ink cherries will be popped, cupcakes will be consumed, and the hazards and enhancements of boob bling will be pondered.

Worlds collide when the hockey boys pay a visit to Inked Armor, the renowned Chicago tattoo studio where master artists Hayden Stryker and Chris Zelter ply their trade. Don't miss the resulting action and insights in this Pucked series and Clipped Wings crossover novella.

PRAISE FOR HELENA HUNTING'S NOVELS

"Characters that will touch your heart and a romance that will leave you breathless."

-*New York Times* bestselling author Tara Sue Me

"Gut wrenching, sexy, twisted, dark, incredibly erotic and a love story like no other. On my all-time favorites list."

-Alice Clayton, *New York Times* bestselling author of *Wallbanger* and The Redhead series

"A look into the world of tattoos and piercings, a dash of humor and a feel-good ending will delight fans and new readers alike."

-*Publishers Weekly* (on *Inked Armor*)

"A unique, deliciously hot, endearingly sweet, laugh out loud, fantastically good time romance!! . . . I loved every single page!!"

—*New York Times* Bestselling author Emma Chase on *PUCKED*

"Sigh inducing swoony and fanning myself sexy. All the stars!"

-*USA Today* bestselling author Daisy Prescott on The Pucked Series

"A hot rollercoaster of a ride!"

-Julia Kent, *New York Times* and *USA Today* bestselling author on *Pucked Over*

"*Pucked Over* is Helena Hunting's funniest and sexiest book yet. SCORCHING HOT with PEE INDUCING LAUGHS. All hail the Beaver Queen."

-T. M. Frazier, *USA Today* bestselling author

TITLES BY HELENA HUNTING

PUCKED SERIES

Pucked (Pucked #1)

Pucked Up (Pucked #2)

Pucked Over (Pucked #3)

Forever Pucked (Pucked #4)

Pucked Under (Pucked #5)

Pucked Off (Pucked #6)

AREA 51: Deleted Scenes & Outtakes

Get Inked (A crossover novella)

THE CLIPPED WINGS SERIES

Cupcakes and Ink

Clipped Wings

Between the Cracks

Inked Armor

Cracks in the Armor

Fractures in Ink

STANDALONE NOVELS

The Librarian Principle

Felony Ever After

Shacking Up

Getting Down (novella)

Hooking Up

I Flipping Love You (May 2018)

The Good Luck Charm (August 2018)

HELENA HUNTING

Published by Helena Hunting

Cover art design by Shannon Lumetta
Cover font from Imagex Fonts
Cover image from Depositphoto.com
Back cover image from Depositphoto.com
Formatting by CP Smith
Editing by Jessica Royer Ocken
Proofing by Marla at Proofing with Style

ISBN: 978-0-9950852-8-2

ACKNOWLEDGMENTS

Mr. Lohgnhorn, I love you. Thanks for being so awesome all the time.

Mom, Dad, Mel and Chris, you're the best kind of family. Pepper, turkey and avacado forever.

Kimberly, you're magic and I'm honoured to be on this journey with you.

Jenn, one day I will be super organized, it just won't be today.

Jessica thank you for straightening out my crooked edges.

Shannon you're like the Harry Potter of cover magic.

Teeny, I'm not sure why you put up with me, but I'm sure glad you do.

Sarah—thanks for sticking around even when I forget my own name.

Hustlers, you're an awesome team and I always feel so incredible fortunate to have all of you!

Beavers and Wood, I wouldn't laugh nearly as much without all of you.

To my Backdoor Babes; Tara, Meghan, Deb and Katherine, I'm grateful none of us are sane.
To my Pams, the Filets, my Nap girls; 101'ers, my Holiday's and

Indies Tijan, Vi, Penelope, Susi, Deb, Erika, Katherine, Alice, Shalu, Amanda, Leisa, Kellie, Kelly, Melissa, Sarah, Tracey, Teeny, Nina, Melanie—you are fabulous in ways I can't explain. Thank you for being my friends, my colleagues, my supporters, my teachers, my cheerleaders and my soft places to land.

To my friends outside of the writing community who love me even though I'm stuck in my own head half the time, thank you for being so amazing and supporting me on this journey.
To all my author friends and colleagues; I'm so fortunate to have such an amazing support system in this crazy, awesome industry.

To all the amazing bloggers and readers out there who have supported me from the beginning of my angst, to the ridiculous of my humour; thank you for loving these stories, for giving them a voice, for sharing your thoughts and for being such amazing readers. I'm honoured and humbled and constantly amazed by what a generous community you are.

To my Originals; my fandom friends who were with me back in the day when Wednesday postings were the way of things, thank you for giving me the gift of your feedback and your excitement. It's such an honour and a joy to know that you're still with me, on this road and that you're reason I took this journey in the first place.

DEDICATION

To Jessica, the editor who edits angst and puckers like none other. But seriously, you're the best.

Get INKED

1

DESIGNS

LILY

Randy's on the couch stroking Wiener. Not *his* wiener, but the wiener we're dog-sitting for the weekend. Sunny's been having some trouble sleeping thanks to being pregnant, so we're taking Wiener off their hands for a few days. Also, Randy loves dogs, and so do I.

Wiener sits to Randy's left, making little whimpery noises while he alternates between patting Wiener's butt and scratching under his chin. Meanwhile, he's using his free hand to flip through a magazine in his lap. Randy, I mean. Not Wiener.

I flop down beside him, fully expecting it to be hockey-related, since Randy's a professional hockey player and all. Except it's not. It's a tattoo magazine. I curl into his side, checking out the designs along with him. Some are pretty and colorful, others are dark and macabre. Randy's mostly a landscape and nature guy, based on his sleeve, but there's a lot of empty canvas, so maybe he's looking to diversify.

"Is this for entertainment or research purposes?" I ask.

The Vagina Emporium really, really likes the idea of Randy adding to his ink. She's already preparing to open the doors and give him an all-access pass based on the thought alone. I didn't put on underwear before I pulled on my sleep shorts, so it isn't going to be much of a problem.

Randy folds the page over and flips to the next one. "Me and the guys planned to get some ink together a while ago. I have a consult with my artist, 'cause I'm thinking about incorporating it into a new sleeve, and he's got a few design ideas he wants to go over."

"Oh?" I remember Randy and Miller talking about tattoos last week, but I didn't think anything of it because, well, Randy has an arm full of them. I look over at his sleeve, and that warm feeling spreads from between my legs through my whole body. "Another sleeve?"

He stops leafing through the magazine to look at me. "Are you okay with that?"

At first I think he's kidding, and then I realize he's actually quite serious.

"Are you asking for permission?" I glance at the flower on his right hand. His dominant hand. His fingering hand. "Or just my blessing?" I try really hard not to sound all breathy and excited.

"Is this you giving it?" He's wearing an odd expression. I'm not sure where he's going with this, but I'll play along.

"Why would you even need it? It's your skin." I trace the outline of a tree on his forearm. "You can put whatever you want on it."

His smirk makes an appearance. "So you're cool with me starting another sleeve?"

He knows I like the tattoos. I trace them all the time with my fingers, and sometimes my tongue, which is exactly what I want to do right now. "Why wouldn't I be cool with it?"

"I don't know. Maybe one sleeve is enough? Maybe you only tolerate my ink because you love me."

I snort. "Your tattoos have nothing to do with why I love you. They're just a bonus."

I wasn't even really a tattoo lover until I met Randy last August. And it isn't that I didn't like tattoos before then; I'd just never understood the obsession with them. Then Randy had come slamming his way into a bathroom while I was shaving my legs, with his tattooed hand shoved down the front of his shorts. As enraged and embarrassed as I'd been, I'd still noticed how hot he was—especially his tattooed arm.

After being with him for the better part of a year, I have a serious appreciation for ink. Particularly his. So much so that I've even entertained getting a tattoo myself. Not a sleeve or anything, just something small and pretty and meaningful. At least to start.

I keep following the outline of the forest on his forearm until I reach the crook of his elbow. It's a sensitive place on Randy, as is the inside of his arm close to his biceps. Sometimes when I'm horny and he's distracted by game highlights, I'll start tracing the designs there. It's usually enough to bring his focus around to where it belongs: Me.

"Wanna guess which one's my favorite?"

"You have a favorite?"

I nod, then tug on the bottom of his shirt.

"What're you doing?"

"What does it look like I'm doing? I can't show you my favorite tattoo when half of them are covered by your shirt." I'm full of shit. Most of his tattoos are visible, except for the ones on his shoulder. But now that we're talking about tattoos and I'm thinking about how much I love the way his arm looks when he's using his fingers to get me off, or holding on to my boob when he takes me from behind, I figure getting closer to naked is a good plan.

"Oh. Well, then." He raises his arms over his head. The sudden movement startles Wiener. He barks and jumps off the couch, pacing around Randy's feet before he trots off.

I take advantage of the newly available space and straddle Randy's thighs. He's already sporting a semi. It's straining against his pajama pants. The elastic waist is super convenient. I lift his shirt, exposing the defined ridges of his abs until his man nipples come into view. I might run into those with my nails, just to watch his abs flex.

Randy's body is insane. He's all cut lines and lean muscle. He's put on a little weight since it's off-season and his workout schedule is a lot lighter, so he's a bit bulkier right now.

I, on the other hand, am struggling to keep my weight from dropping thanks to Randy's ultra-high sex drive. Apparently when he's not expending energy on the ice, he needs to find a way to get rid of it. Getting freaky with me happens to be one of his preferred ways.

I pull the shirt over his head and toss it to the floor. I've messed up his beard and hair on purpose so I can perform one of my favorite pre-sex activities. Before Randy can fix his face, I run my fingers through his hair, and then smooth out his beard with my fingernails.

He makes this deep sound in his throat, somewhere between a man-purr and a growl, as he runs his palms up my bare legs, stopping just before the hem of my shorts. So I keep stroking his beard a while longer.

When I stop, he grabs my wrists. "You should keep doing that."

I lean in until I can feel his hard-on between my legs. It's not a semi anymore. Now it's a fully. "I thought we were talking about my favorite tattoo," I whisper, my lips close to his.

"I thought that was a bullshit excuse to get my shirt off."

"That's because all you think about is sex and hockey."

"Not true. I have other thoughts."

"Such as?" I drop a kiss on his neck, right where his beard ends.

"Such as how long it's going to take for you to stop pretending you're not ogling my chest."

"You're pretty full of yourself, aren't you?"

"Not as full as you're going to be pretty fucking soon." He slips his hands under my shirt.

I clamp my elbows against my ribs to prevent him from getting it over my head. "Oh? You think so, eh?"

Since I'm barring his way under my shirt, he goes for my shorts instead. "Are you even wearing panties?"

"We're not talking about my wardrobe choices right now; we're talking about my favorite tattoo." I don't stop him from feeling his way around in there, but much to my vagina's disappointment, as well as the rest of me, he doesn't make a move to verify my lack of panties.

"You should hurry up and do that so I can tell you about all my favorite Lily parts."

"Don't you want to guess?" I run my fingers through his hair one more time, skimming the short sides with my pinkies. Even his hair is sexy.

"Sure. If it gets us past this part of your foreplay faster."

"Who says this is even going to lead to sex? Maybe I just feel like talking tonight."

Randy's brow lifts, then furrows. "You're kidding, right?"

I slow-blink at him and give him my best fake-confused face. "Just because I'm sitting in your lap and you have your shirt off doesn't mean we have to get totally naked."

He nods somberly, but I can tell he doesn't buy it for a second. And he shouldn't. "Of course not. You can wear your shorts if you want to, even if that makes it more difficult for me."

I snicker and follow the contour of his abs down to the waistband of his pants. I take my time, because—as stated earlier—Randy's abs are incredible. He has the most amazing six-pack in the world. I like it best when it's flexed, either because I'm riding him or he's riding me.

"How about if you guess right, I have to do whatever you want tonight, but if you guess wrong, you have to do whatever I want?"

He's focused on my fingers, which are trailing back and forth along the waistband of his pants. His eyes lift, his expression devious. "If I guess right, I get whatever I want?"

"Within reason."

I can practically see his wheels turning. "Just to be clear, we're talking about sex, right?"

"Sex? I was talking about board games. I was thinking Monopoly would be fun. You know how that can go on forever and ever."

Randy grabs me by the waist and flips me over so I'm sprawled on the couch. I don't have time to get my legs closed before he gets between them and stretches out on top of me.

I put my hands on his chest and push, but he's heavy. "Hey! We're having a conversation, remember?"

"There will be no Monopoly tonight," he growls.

"There will be if you guess wrong," I threaten.

He pushes up so he's doing a one-armed plank. Holding his tattooed hand in front of my face he wiggles his fingers. "I'm going to say this one."

"You're so smart." I lift my head enough to bite one of his knuckles. "Do you know why it's my favorite?"

"Because it's like I have your name tattooed on my hand?" The flower is a lily. Since we started dating, I've come to discover it's his mother's favorite, and that's why it's there. But I like that there's an unintentional connection to me, and that sometimes people come to the inaccurate conclusion that he had it put there because it represents me.

"If I say yes, does that make me egotistical?" I'm working really hard to keep my legs from wrapping around his waist.

Randy's tongue peeks out to sweep across his bottom lip. "Not even a little."

"Good to know, but that's not the primary reason it's my favorite." I press my knees against his hips, but keep my feet glued to the couch.

"No?"

"Nope."

Randy runs his hand down my side and gives my thigh a gentle squeeze. "You gonna tell me why, or are you gonna keep me guessing?"

"I like that you're this big, badass hockey player with a pretty tattoo right on the back of your hand. It's sexy."

"Oh, yeah?"

"Mmm." I bite my lip, being intentionally coy. "Wanna know why else I love that tattoo?"

"Why's that?" Randy drops his hips so his amazing hard-on is now pressed against my stomach.

"'Cause it looks hot when that hand is between my thighs."

"Is that right?"

"It is."

"You mean like this?" Randy pushes up, folding back on his knees between my spread legs.

I'm momentarily disheartened by the lack of moody dick contact. Moody dick is my nickname for Randy's penis. He took a skate to the groin as a kid, resulting in a pretty significant scar that makes his penis look sad when it's soft and happy when it's hard. He slips his fingers into the front of my shorts—thank Christ for the elastic waist—yanks them down low, and grazes my clit with his knuckle.

I suck in a sharp breath. "Just like that."

He withdraws his hand just as fast as he shoved it down there. "I knew you weren't wearing panties."

"Why bother when there's a good chance you're going to take them off anyway?"

Randy eases his hands up the inside of my thighs, stopping too far away for anything good to happen. "I thought you wanted to play board games tonight."

"Naked board games?"

"The board games part is where you lose me." He's still kneeling between my parted legs.

I open them even farther. "How about just playing naked?"

He grabs the crotch of my shorts—with his tattooed hand, of course—and makes a fist. At first I think he's going to yank them off, which would be totally welcome at this point. Sometimes I threaten no naked time just to amp Randy up. Not that it's necessary, he's usually pretty amped as it is. But the sex when he's been worried he isn't getting any is often out of this world.

Instead of taking off my shorts, he tightens his fist. His lip curls in a sexy sneer as he rubs his knuckles over my clit again. I groan and start to lift my hips, but he's quick to put his free palm low on my stomach, keeping me from achieving any additional friction. This is Randy's way of punishing me for my threats, even if he knows it was all a farce.

"Why don't you take your shirt off for me, luscious?" He adjusts his grip, his knuckles pressing right where I want them.

Grabbing the bottom, I keep my eyes on his and drag the

cotton up over my abs. Like Randy, I have a six-pack—mine is far less defined, but it's definitely there. Randy's eyes are on my stomach, moving higher as I uncover more skin. I may arch my back a little more than necessary as I expose the swell of my breasts. I don't have big boobs, so the arching helps make them look more ample. It also makes Randy's knuckles slide over the right spot.

My nipples pop out, and I may or may not drag my fingernails over them and moan rather loudly—for effect, of course. Randy huffs out a small laugh because he knows my game. His lips part, that smirky smirk of his still making the top one curl. I'm in for some amazing orgasms tonight. I'm already on the brink of one thanks to the teasing.

Now, let me be clear on something—prior to Randy, it used to take some work for me to have an orgasm. Whether it was with someone else or on my own, I required at least a good ten minutes of direct stimulation to reach that amazing state of bliss. But something about our particular brand of chemistry has changed that. I don't know if our pheromones are in perfect sync, or we're orgasm soul mates, or some other kind of soul mates, but all Randy has to do is look at me the right way, and I'm halfway to coming. It's insane. I'm not complaining, though.

Randy runs the hand on my lower abs up over my stomach to palm my left breast. He captures the nipple between his fingers, then leans over me so he can take the other one between his lips. His soft beard tickles my skin, and the pressure between my legs increases. He's now hovering over me, and it's a lot of sensation. Everywhere.

He lifts his eyes as he flat-tongues my nipple, just like he'd do if his face was between my legs instead. His grin is pure evil when he closes his mouth over the tight peak and does the magic swirl with his tongue. I gasp and shudder when I feel his teeth.

9

"You're getting close, aren't you?" His voice is muffled by my boob, but I still understand.

"Uh-huh."

He circles my clit, and I'm done. I try to lift my hips, but I can't do much with the way he's partly on top of me. It doesn't matter anyway, since I'm coming like I haven't had an orgasm in a week. In reality, it's been less than sixteen hours. We had sex before I went to work this morning. Like I said, Randy likes to get his fuck on. A lot.

He releases my nipple from his mouth and sits back on his knees again. "That sounded like it felt good."

"So good," I mumble. "You should give me another."

"You think so, huh?" He captures my still-sensitive clit between two knuckles.

I jolt with the sensation, lifting my hips off the couch with a yelp.

"Too much?" He doesn't take the pressure off, waiting for my reply instead.

I shake my head and take a few deep breaths.

"I don't think I'm gonna take these off when I fuck you."

Goose bumps break out across my skin at his words and the expression on his pretty, rugged, sexy face. "Whatever you want, baby."

"That's right. I guessed right, so I get whatever I want." His honey eyes drop to where he's still fisting the crotch of my shorts. "How long you think you can hold this position?"

With my shoulders and head resting on one cushion I'm sort of doing a half-bridge. It's a lot easier on the floor where I have a hard, stable surface as opposed to the couch, but I'm sure I can hold it for as long as I need to if more orgasms and moody dick are involved.

Sometimes Randy and I have plank-offs. Whoever wins gets

oral. I'm up to six minutes now. I'm pretty sure I can hold this position at least that long. But it really depends on what's at stake.

"As long as you need me to," I say.

Randy's grin is all devious sexiness. "Good answer, 'cause the longer you hold it, the more you get to come."

My clit throbs at the mention of coming. Oh, sweet Jesus, Randy's on a mission tonight. I don't point out that he's the winner, so he should probably be the one having all the orgasms. He hasn't mastered the male multiple O yet, so I'm happy to manage that situation until he does.

Randy lets go of my shorts, which also means his knuckles are no longer pinching my clit. I make a sad sound, which quickly becomes a groan when he fists his extra-hard cock and gives it a stroke.

"I'm pretty sure these shorts are screwed." He slips a finger through what I imagine is stretched-out material. However, I can't see it because my head is way lower than my crotch.

"I guess so, since you're about to screw me while I'm wearing them."

Randy rubs the head of his cock over my clit. It's like a jolt of electricity is shooting through my body, and its end point is his incredible penis. I make some kind of unintelligible sound or word, or a sound and word combined. And then his magic cock is gone and the noise I'm making isn't a happy one.

"I forgot to do something important." Randy crouches down and grabs my left ass cheek—I assume he may still be fisting his cock with his right hand.

The hot press of his tongue against my clit makes me gasp, but the slow stroke up makes me moan. Then Randy does the one thing guaranteed to make me come fast and hard. He doesn't swirl his tongue or lick me like I'm an ice cream cone he wants to savor. Oh no. Randy flattens his tongue against my clit and starts sucking. I have no idea why this feels as good as it does, but every time it sends me right over the edge.

He doesn't stop there, though, because this is Randy Ballistic we're talking about, and he can go forever when he wants to. Also, he likes to torture me with orgasms sometimes, and tonight seems to be one of those nights. Instead of giving me some time to recover, he keeps sucking. So of course I try to escape his suctioning mouth by dropping my hips.

He releases my clit with a pop, and his beard skims over the sensitive skin. "Nuh-uh, remember what I said about holding this position?"

I give him a bleary-eyed, questioning look, because I can barely remember my own damn name right now.

"The longer you hold it, the more you get to come."

"I didn't think you were actually serious."

"Oh, I'm serious." To prove how serious he is, he re-suctions his mouth to my clit and resumes sucking until I come again.

I have no idea how long I've been holding this position, but my legs are shaking, and I've got a serious head rush going on. Randy gets back on his knees between my legs, returning to his previous torture of cock-to-clit rubbing. When I'm close to coming again, he slides low and eases inside. Just the head, though.

At this point the muscles in my thighs are burning, and I feel a calf cramp coming on, but I'm determined to make it through the sexing in this damn position, because if I do, the next time we play this game, and I get whatever I want, I'm going to make him do some kind of acrobatic stunt. Randy uses one hand to keep the crotch of my stretched-out shorts pulled out of the way so he can watch while he eases inside me.

"You look so fucking hot right now, luscious."

"You should take a picture," I suggest.

Randy looks around for his phone, but it's not on the coffee table. "Fuck. My phone is charging." For a second it seems like he's debating whether to stop what he's doing and get it, or fuck it and keep going.

He chooses the latter, which is definitely preferable considering how long I've been doing a half-bridge on the couch and also how much I'd like all of his dick inside me, not just the head. Randy smooths his tattooed hand up my thigh and pushes inside.

I groan, partly because it feels good and also because I'm trying to lift my hips farther and my quads feel like they're on fire. Randy takes a little bit of pressure off when he holds my right hip, but it's not enough to alleviate the burn, which is becoming an orgasm distraction. Though I have had three already, and he's only going to have one. This round, anyway.

The biggest issue is that the couch, as comfy as it may be for lying-down sex, isn't all that practical for acrobatic sex. Randy's learning this as he tries to pick up thrusting momentum but struggles with the uneven, soft surface.

It's fine with me. It still feels good, and watching him try to troubleshoot the issue while keeping me in this goddamn position is actually entertaining, even if it is becoming close to unbearably uncomfortable. But I refuse to be the one to break.

His frustration is the first to give out. He grunts his annoyance, hooks his arms under my knees, palms my ass, and leans forward. "Grab my shoulders and hold on tight."

I do exactly as he asks—it's whatever he wants tonight—and I'm suddenly in motion. My shoulders hit the back of the couch as Randy's feet land on the floor.

"What exactly are you doing?"

"Changing things up," he says, like our sex-robatics should

be expected.

To a certain degree they are. Randy likes to try new positions, but this is a little over the top. I'm parallel to the seat of the couch rather than laid out on it now, with my shoulders resting where my head would be if I were sitting and, you know, watching TV or something. I let my head drop back so I'm looking at an upside-down version of myself in the mirror on the wall.

I have a very clear view of Randy's beautifully built, straining muscles as he holds me perpendicular to his body. He's angling me perfectly so that my boobs don't impede his view of my shorts in the mirror—they really are horribly stretched out now—and the base of his cock as he pulls out a little and pushes back in.

Well, this explains everything.

"Just can't help yourself, can you? Always wanting to watch what you're doing to me."

He shifts his gaze from his own reflection to mine. "You don't seem to be minding the view."

I grab my boob and bite my lip, still keeping my eyes on him. "I love the view."

It's really all I need to say. Randy holds on to my hips and pounds two more orgasms out of me before he lifts me up and carries me piggyfront—with his cock still inside me—to our bedroom where he sexes me until he finally has his own orgasm.

We didn't even bother to pull the covers down, so we lie on top of the duvet, breathing heavily. Randy rolls us so we're side by side. I trace the lines of a high-rise on his arm while I come down from the orgasm high.

"Can I come with you tomorrow?" I ask.

"To the consult with my tattoo artist?"

I glance up at him. "Would that be okay?"

"Sure. I mean, I'm just going to be looking at designs and

going over plans. It's nothing exciting."

"I don't have to come if you don't want me to."

Randy brushes my damp bangs off my forehead. "You can come if you want. My artist is a little intense, though."

"Intense how?" Violet mentioned having gone with Alex when he got his most recent tattoo at the end of the season. I'm not sure his artist was the same as Randy's. But she said all the guys there were hot.

"I don't know. Hayden's like...serious most of the time."

"So I shouldn't make jokes about spelling things wrong?"

Randy makes a face. "Probably not."

"Noted." I do some more finger tracing. "Maybe I should get something, too."

"You want a tattoo?" I'm pretty sure his voice lowers an octave.

I shrug and follow the outline into the crease of his arm. "I have some ideas."

He raises an eyebrow. "Do you now?"

"Why do you sound so surprised?"

"You only have regular earrings. You don't really seem like the body-modification type." He skims the shell of my ear. I'm wearing the earrings he bought me for Valentine's Day. They're mismatched skates: one is a black hockey skate, the other a white figure skate. I pretty much wear them all the time.

"Maybe I've just never had an opportunity to explore my wild side."

"I'm pretty sure we explore your wild side every time we have sex in a public bathroom."

"We haven't done that in months!"

"Uh...the last time we were at Sunny and Miller's, we totally fucked in their bathroom."

"That was attached to the bedroom we were sleeping in; it

doesn't count." I pinch him, and he laughs.

"You can talk to Hayden about your idea tomorrow if there's time," he says. "Maybe he can sketch something for you."

I caress his forearm. His tight, hard forearm. The forearm attached to the hand attached to the fingers that recently ruined my shorts. "He's done all your work so far, right?"

"Mmm-hmm." Randy watches my fingers crawling up his arm. "He has. He's a seriously gifted artist. You should see the wings he put on his girlfriend's back. They're insane."

"Insane how?"

"Like, they look real. He's got pictures in his custom album so you can check them out tomorrow." Randy traces an imaginary pattern on my arm. "So if you got a tattoo, where would you want it?"

I lift a shoulder and let it fall. "I don't know. There are a few spots I wouldn't mind."

He peruses my naked body. "Such as?"

"Well, I thought about maybe my shoulder." I tap the area just beside my blade.

He kisses where my finger just was, following with a nibble and a ticklish beard rub. "It's a sexy spot, for sure. Any other ideas?" His very recently used cock kicks against my thigh where it's been resting since it left the Vagina Emporium.

Interesting. Talking about me getting a tattoo seems to be making Randy randy again.

"I could put one on my ankle or my foot; that way I can cover it if I want to, but it'll be visible in the summer when I'm wearing open-toed shoes and sandals." I run my foot along the outside of Randy's thigh.

"I like that idea. Tattoos on the top of your foot can be painful, and sometimes the ink bleeds."

"Hmm. I didn't think about that. Well, there's always the hip.

I mean, I guess it's kind of cliché, but it's sexy, right?"

Randy drags a finger over my ribs and down my side, stopping at my hip where a potential, yet-to-be-designed tattoo might go. "That would definitely be a sexy place for some ink."

"It sounds like there's a but in there."

"It could be painful, what with you being so lean and all." Randy's way of calling me skinny is so much nicer than the way the jealous girls used to say it when I was a kid.

I reach down and give his semi-hard cock a pat. "It might be worth the pain if this is the kind of reaction it gets."

"You think so?" He rolls over on top of me, fitting himself between my legs again.

"Wow. I didn't realize you'd be this excited about me getting a tattoo."

Randy hooks my leg over his hip. "You have no fucking idea."

Based on the smoulder he's got going on, and the big hard-on now mashed against my stomach, I think I do, in fact, have a fucking idea.

Round two is even better than round one. Now I'm really excited to meet his tattoo artist, and not just because Violet said he's hot.

SINCE WHEN DO YOU LIKE HOCKEY?

HAYDEN

I pat my back pocket, checking for my wallet for the seventeenth time as I round the corner. "I gotta roll out, kitten. I've got a consult this morning."

I'm greeted by a sight that immediately makes me reconsider whether I need to go in almost two hours early on a Saturday morning. Tenley, my girlfriend, is wearing my favorite outfit in the entire world: a pair of shorts that are far too skimpy for her to ever leave the house in, and a camisole that shows off some of the design I put on her back. But that's not the best part. It's the apron and the hot pink legwarmers slouched around her ankles that make my dick try to punch its way through my zipper.

That and the fact that she's making cupcakes. I fucking love cupcakes almost as much as I love Tenley.

She looks over her shoulder, her long, dark ponytail swishing. She's holding up a spatula covered in fresh buttercream icing. "It's only nine. I thought you didn't have to be at the shop until eleven."

"I'm going in early to set up."

"For a consult?"

"It's an important client." I haven't told Tenley who's coming in, mostly because I don't think she'll actually care. She's not a sporty girl, so I don't expect her to get all excited about a hockey player getting a tattoo.

She cocks her head to the side. "Who's so important that you have to go in this early?"

"I have an NHL player coming in. I usually schedule his appointments early so it's not a thing, you know?"

Tenley perks up a little. "An NHL player? For Chicago?"

"Yeah." I take her hand and curl all but her index finger into a fist. Then I swipe it over the spatula.

"Which player?" she asks as I bring her finger to my mouth.

"Ballistic." I suck the creamy sugar off, swirling my tongue to make sure I got it all.

"Randy Ballistic?" She yanks her finger away, her eyes going wide. "You have a consult with *Randy Ballistic*?"

"Uh, yeah." I go for the spatula, but she hides it behind her back. It's not much of a deterrent. In fact, it allows me to pin her against the counter.

"I can't believe this is the first time you've mentioned it! And you're meeting with him today?" Tenley's voice is all pitchy.

I pause in my quest to get the icing from her. "Since when do you like hockey?"

"Are you kidding? Who doesn't like hockey?"

"You're always reading something when I put sports on."

"I can multitask."

I'm not sure I believe her, but her face is going red. "What's his number?"

She grins. "Sixty-nine."

"What position does he play?"

"He's a forward, and he played for New York before he was traded here last year. Chicago only made it through the first round of finals, and their team captain, Alex Waters, suffered a serious concussion and some broken ribs in March, which took him out for the rest of the season."

"Who are you, and what the fuck have you done with my girlfriend?"

Tenley pokes me in the chest. "Just because I'm a book nerd doesn't mean I can't appreciate highly aggressive sports."

"Apparently."

Her other hand also disappears behind her back, which pushes her chest out. If she wasn't wearing the cupcake-patterned apron, I'd be able to see some cleavage. When her hand reappears, she holds her index finger in front of my face. It's covered in icing. I latch on to her wrist and wrap my lips around it. The only thing I like better than Tenley's cupcakes with buttercream icing is Tenley decorated with buttercream icing. It makes for sticky, but fun and delicious sex.

"Do you think I'd be able to meet him?"

I'm still sucking on her finger, so I'm hoping the breathless quality of her voice is related to what I'm doing, rather than thoughts of Randy. I take my time tongue-cleaning her finger before I let it go. "Only if you keep it together and don't act all starstruck."

"I won't act starstruck." She sounds a little offended.

I give her a look.

Tenley purses her lips. "Seriously. I will keep it together."

"Okay. Why don't you come by the shop when you're done with the cupcake business."

Her grin is ridiculous. She jumps up and down, her boobs bouncing. "Oh my God! Yay!"

"On second thought, maybe it's not a good idea." I'm sort

of teasing. Tenley never gets girly excited over anything apart from maybe when I take her to concerts, so this kind of reaction makes me a little wary. Because I get jealous like that.

It's something I'm working on.

Based on my current reaction, I'm still not quite where I need to be.

"I promise I'll get all my excitement out before I get to the shop."

"Should I be worried about how jacked up you are over this?" I steal the spatula from her and lick it, heedless of her protest.

Tenley skims my arm and curves one palm around the back of my neck. "Are you getting territorial on me?"

"Should I?"

She cocks a brow. "That depends."

"On what?"

"On what I get out of it."

"You mean besides meeting a famous hockey player?"

Tenley twirls the end of her ponytail around her finger and runs it along the column of her neck. She's taunting me. On purpose. I lean in and brush my lips along the edge of her jaw. "I have to leave for work."

"Okay. We can talk about this later."

I bite the sensitive skin just below her ear. She tastes sweet, like the sugar she's been feeding into the mixer. I move down an inch and suck just a little.

"Hayden," Tenley grabs my shoulders.

"Hmm?" I move an inch lower and suck again, harder this time.

Instead of getting annoyed at me for possibly giving her a hickey, Tenley grabs my hair, keeping my mouth attached to her neck. "Don't start something you're not going to finish."

I chuckle and glance at the clock on the stove. It's only ten after nine. I can take care of her and still get to the shop with plenty of time to prep. I left everything out on my desk last night anyway. It's just me being anal, partly because Randy's consult will be followed by a group meeting in a couple of weeks. He and a few teammates are getting similar versions of the same tattoo. I want everything perfect for when the guys come in to review their designs.

I pull the tie on her apron, and Tenley ducks her chin so I can get it over her head. Her nipple shields are visible through her flimsy tank. Before I take that off, I reach behind her and pull down the blinds, keeping the neighbors across the way from getting a view of the action. Tenley helps out by dropping her shorts and kicking them across the floor.

I grab her by the hips and lift her onto the counter.

"There's only ten minutes before I have to test the cupcakes," she warns.

"I'll be fast."

"Not too fast."

I pull her tank over her head and groan. Cupping her breasts, I thumb her nipples. "Did you change these this morning?" She has on my favorite shields: cupcakes with little jeweled barbells. They make her nipples look permanently hard.

"I did."

"I fucking *love* these." I lean in and take one between my lips, then move to the other side, giving the other nipple the same treatment while Tenley fumbles with my belt and the zipper on my jeans.

Before she can stick her hands down my pants, I drop to my knees, dragging her forward until she's at the edge of the counter. Tenley holds tight to the granite lip, her head resting on the cabinets behind her, waiting for my next move.

Starting at her knee I kiss a slow, wet path up the inside of her thigh. I pause at the tiny cupcake tattoo I put just above the crest of her pelvis. I'm the only one who gets to see it.

Dropping my head, I brush my lips over her clit and flick her with my tongue. She jerks and sighs, but doesn't say anything about wanting me to go faster. Tenley knows the more demanding she is, the longer I'm likely to draw out the torture. It always ends well for her, but we're under some time constraints. Based on the timer on the stove, I'm down to six and a half minutes to make her come.

That shouldn't be a problem.

I suck softly on the barbell piercing the hood of her clit before pressing my tongue flat against it. My tongue ring clinks faintly against her barbell, and Tenley moans. I lift her feet onto my shoulders and keep up the hard licks, interspersed with light sucking and tongue swirls. She likes it all based on the moans and hair pulling.

I check the timer. I'm down to a minute and a half. "You better come soon, kitten, or the cupcakes are gonna burn."

"You're the one who loses if that happens. Maybe you should lick faster."

She has a point. Still, I can't let her get away with that kind of snark unpunished. I grab her hips and hold on so she can't get away as I press the ball of my tongue ring hard against her clit and make tight circles. Tenley gasps and tries to bow forward, but there isn't room for that to happen. Instead she's forced to hold on to the cabinet pulls for balance.

"Holy fuuuuuck." She starts bucking just as the timer goes off.

When the hip jerking stops and she goes limp, I push up off my knees and grab her tank top from the counter, using it to wipe my mouth. "Want me to check the cupcakes, kitten?"

She makes a noise rather than using an actual word, but I

take it as a yes. I wash my hands before I shove them into the mitts and open the oven. The sweet aroma of fresh vanilla makes my mouth water instantly. These aren't some Betty Crocker mix knockoffs. These are from scratch.

I use the tester thing, making sure it comes out clean before I take the cakes out and set them on the counter to cool.

Tenley's still slouched against the cabinets with her legs splayed when I turn back to her. Since I didn't use my fingers to warm her up, she's decided to use her own. She has three buried in her perfect pussy, eyes locked on me as I pull my shirt over my head, drape it neatly over a chair, and then shove my pants and boxer briefs over my hips.

I give my cock a couple of strokes, ready to replace those fingers and chase down my own orgasm. "Looking for this, kitten?"

At my approach, Tenley removes her fingers and opens her legs wider. "Uh-huh."

Since foreplay's already been taken care of, I circle her clit with the head of my cock. The ball on the barbell that goes through one side and comes out the other makes a dull clink against her clit piercing. Tenley pushes my hand out of the way, wrapping her slick fingers around me. She's the one who drags the head lower and slides a little closer to the edge of the counter, encouraging me to ease inside.

She's still holding the cabinet pull with one hand, her gaze fixed on my cock as the head disappears. Once I'm past the piercing I give it a few seconds for her to adjust before I go any farther.

Her eyes flutter shut and she utters a soft *fuck* when I go deeper. Once I'm all the way in, I cradle her cheek in my palm, fingers slipping into the hair at the nape of her neck.

Tenley tips her head up so I have access to her mouth. She

sucks my bottom lip, then sweeps my mouth with her tongue, and I meet her stroke in a slow, warm tangle. I don't move for a good minute or more, savoring the way it feels when she's wrapped around me like this. This woman is my everything.

Tenley digs her heel into my ass, a sure sign she wants some friction. I pull out, maybe halfway, and ease back in.

She moans my name, running her hands over my shoulders and into my hair. The way she grips it is a litmus test for what she wants, and how hard she wants it. I'm more inclined to go easy on her, based on our location—granite counters aren't very forgiving—but a change of position can make all the difference.

I slide my hands up the outside of her thighs, feeling the raised scar on her leg from the accident she was in before we met. Pulling her even closer to the edge, I reverse the motion until the crook of my arms meets the back of her knees. "This okay?"

She nods and pulls her knees up higher so her toes touch the counter.

"You sure? It's not uncomfortable?"

"It's perfect, and it'll be so much better when you really start moving."

So I do, with long, slow strokes we can both watch thanks to her angle and the way I keep her open for me. She slips two fingers into her mouth, then lowers them, rubbing circles on her clit that pick up speed as I do.

The pulse of her orgasm hits me as she lets out a soft moan, and then I come, hard and fast, pulling her tight against me while my vision blurs and sensation rules my world for a few seconds.

When I can do more than just feel again, I ease her legs down slowly, one at a time, and then massage her hips while I kiss her. I'm still inside, because I'm still half hard, and she's warm and snug. If it wasn't already after nine thirty, I might consider taking her back up to bed for another round, but I seriously need to get to the shop.

I need time before my consult to get my head in the game. While I may have put Randy's sleeve on him, that's a lot different than having the entire Inked Armor team work on him and a group of his friends.

Tenley doesn't bother to put her tank back on since I've used it as a towel. She runs off to the bathroom, a slight hitch in her step, probably from being in that cramped position for as long as I had her. I used to feel guilty whenever she limped after sex, or anytime really, but I understand now that it's residual from the accident, and it'll always be that way, no matter how gentle or not gentle I am.

I wash my face and hands in the sink, getting soap in my mouth in the process. It's better than me smelling like my girlfriend's pussy, though. I root through the silverware drawer for a knife and use it to slather two cupcakes in icing while Tenley's still in the bathroom.

I peel the wrapper off the first one and take a huge bite, chewing a couple of times before I shove the rest in. They're the best when they're still warm. Tenley comes back—wearing an entirely new outfit—just as I start on cupcake number two.

"Hayden!"

"What? I'm hungry," I tell her through a mouthful. I doubt she can understand me, but when it comes to cupcakes, I don't think I really need to explain.

"It's too early to eat these!" she scolds.

"It's never too early for cupcakes." I take another giant bite and lean it to kiss her, but she puts a hand in front of my face to prevent me from getting too close.

"Finish chewing first, please."

I do as she asks and go so far as to pour myself a glass of

water to wash it all down. Then I go in for the kiss I want. I throw in a little tongue just because. "Come by the shop when you're done with this, and I'll introduce you to Randy."

"Okay. Do you have a full schedule today?"

"Nope. Just the consult and a couple of sketches to get ready for tomorrow."

She puts her hands on my chest. "So I can have you to myself later?"

"If that's what you want, kitten."

She rises up on her toes and kisses the bottom of my chin. "Yes, please."

I leave before I get another hard-on, which happens often, and head to the shop.

Lisa, our piercer and bookkeeper, is already there when I arrive. Her lavender hair is pulled up into a complicated ponytail. It makes her look like she just stepped off the set of *Leave it to Beaver*. Her dress, which is also lavender, looks like it's from that era as well. The combat boots and tattoos make her look badass, though.

She points her pen at the clock over her head; it's already ten. "I thought you said you'd be here at nine thirty."

"I got distracted."

"Did you now? Does she happen to be five two with dark hair and a thing for baking cupcakes?"

I give her a look, but don't bother to respond. Tenley's always my number one distraction.

Chris, my business partner and one of the other tattoo artists, comes out of the private room with a stack of folders. "Finally decided to show up, huh?"

"Why're you here this early?"

"Because you said you were coming in to show Ballistic the designs, and since I'll be working on more than one of those guys, I figured it'd be good to be here in case he has any questions about the ones I sketched."

"But the rest of the guys from the team aren't coming in for at least a couple of weeks."

Chris shrugs. "I just wanna be prepared. It's kind of a big deal to be working on these guys."

He's got a point. I've done Randy's sleeve, and Chris has put a couple of pieces on Waters, the team captain, but now we're designing tattoos that are variations on a similar theme, and Chris will be modifying a design that's already on Waters' arm. It's a cool project, and it'll be even cooler when we have five different pieces on five different NHL players. We're also pulling in Jamie, the third tattooist in the shop, to work on one of the guys.

"Tenley's coming by later," I tell Lisa as I pass the folder of preliminary designs over to Chris.

She glances up. "Really? Does she know who your consult is this morning, by chance?"

I stop leafing through Randy's folder. "What?"

"You told her who your consult is?"

"Well, yeah..." I don't get why Lisa suddenly looks all smug.

"You know she thinks he looks kind of like you. Only, you know—" She motions to my face and then the rest of me. "—with a beard and fewer tattoos."

"We don't look alike." I turn to Chris for confirmation.

He shrugs. "I guess I can kinda see it, except you're all Gumby skinny, and he's a tank."

"I'm not fucking skinny," I snap. I turn back to Lisa, since

Chris is no help. "So does Tenley actually like hockey?"

"She likes hockey for the same reason all girls like hockey, Hayden."

"Which is because…"

"It's full of hot guys with lots of stamina."

"I have excellent stamina."

Lisa rolls her eyes. "You sound jealous."

"I'm not jealous." I'm kind of jealous.

She pats my cheek. "I'm messing with you, Hayden. Tenley loves hockey. She knows all the Chicago stats. It's almost creepy."

"Why am I just finding this out now?"

"Maybe because you spend most of your spare time with your tongue in her mouth, and she hasn't had an opportunity to tell you?" Chris offers with a smile.

I don't bother answering. I just take my stuff to the private room where I'm meeting with Randy.

We've learned to do consults with high-profile clients away from the windows, so passing fans, or other clients who are fans, don't turn a half-hour consult into a two-hour fangirl session, which very well may happen anyway with Tenley coming by later.

3

CUPCAKE-WRAPPER PORN

RANDY

No one's sitting at the jewelry counter, which doubles as reception, when we arrive at Inked Armor. The shop is quiet apart from the low tones of rock music filtering through the sound system.

"Why don't you have a look around while we wait?" I tell Lily, who's hanging off my tattooed arm. Mostly I need her to stop touching me so I don't get another hard-on. I had to work to contain one the entire trip over here while she talked about how she really likes the idea of an inner thigh tattoo.

It's my own damn fault since I'm the one who suggested it in the first place.

She lets go of me and wanders around the shop, checking out framed designs on the walls. This isn't like most tattoo shops in the area. The sign out front reads *By appointment only*, and stock designs aren't typical here. Intricate custom pieces in various stages of completion cover the walls. Custom albums labeled with the name of each artist sit on the coffee table. My sleeve is in Hayden's album.

Lisa, the lavender-haired piercer, comes out of the office and squeals her surprise. "Randy! Does Hayden know you're here?"

I smile and lift a hand in greeting. "We're a little early."

She looks over to Lily, who's stopped her perusal to check out the female voice associated with the enthusiastic greeting. Her expression is a mixture of mild shock, awe, and if I'm not mistaken, a hint of jealousy. I like Lily in green. A lot.

"Lisa, this is my girlfriend, Lily. She wanted to come along today and maybe see about Hayden designing a piece for her, too."

"Oh? Awesome!" Lisa clomps across the hardwood floor, her heavy boots a serious contrast to her lavender dress, and extends a hand to Lily, whose lips turn up in a tentative smile. "It's really nice to meet you, Lily."

"You, too."

"Hayden doesn't have appointments scheduled until later this afternoon, so it shouldn't be a problem to discuss a design for you."

"He didn't do that because of me, did he?" I ask.

"You know what he's like. He doesn't want any kind of divided focus. Oh, and Chris is here, too, so you can talk about the team designs, if you want."

"That would be awesome. Hayden mentioned he had some preliminary sketches worked up." My excitement over the new sleeve becomes more real now that I'm here, in the shop.

Hayden comes out of the private room where I had my sleeve done. He's tall and kind of lanky, with full sleeves. His typically serious face breaks into a smile.

"Hey, man! You're early." He holds out his hand, and we shake while bumping shoulders.

"Is that okay? You know how it is when the excitement kinda

takes over."

Hayden pats me on the back. "I got you. I'm getting the itch again, but I'm running out of skin to put it on."

"I've got a long way to go before that happens." I glance over at Lily, who's migrated to the jewelry counter with Lisa.

She's not looking at the contents of the glass case. Her gaze is fixed on us, and it's bouncing from me to Hayden. I motion her over and throw an arm around her shoulder. "This is my girlfriend, Lily. She wanted to come along and maybe talk to you about a design."

Hayden turns his grin on her and extends a hand. "It's great to meet you. We can definitely talk ink designs once we go through Randy's, sound good?"

"That sounds great. Awesome. Thanks. Nice to meet you." Lily shakes his hand a little longer than necessary, her cheeks flushing as she looks over his arms and the lick of vine crawling up his neck.

Hayden takes us to the private room so we won't have any interruptions. He's always super organized—Lisa calls him anal—and he seems to get razzed for it a lot.

He goes into professional artist mode as soon as he flips open the folder. Bright bursts of color decorate the page, and the designs look almost three-dimensional. Hayden's been working with watercolor images lately, and these are fantastic.

"So I know when we first started talking about this, we thought we'd start shoulder down, but I think that really depends on where you plan to get the team tattoo." Hayden flips over another page.

"Oh my God! That's incredible." Lily grabs my arm with one hand and reaches out with the other, but stops abruptly and looks to Hayden. "Can I touch that? It looks so real."

A half-grin quirks up the side of his mouth. "Yeah, go right ahead."

Lily brushes over the design and glances at the naked arm she's stroking. "That's going to look amazing."

"I think so, too." The hockey puck looks as if it's being shot toward the net, a spray of ice framing it. It appears as if it could come flying off the page and hit me in the face. The rest of the tattoos have a similar three-dimensional feel.

Hayden and I quickly get into the fine details, talking about shading, placement, and which designs I like the best.

After half an hour of Lily hanging off my arm, offering her opinions, and bouncing in her seat, I'm about ready to take her home and bang the excitement right out of her. But we still need to talk about her tattoo.

Hayden marks the designs in order of preference and makes notes on the changes we've discussed before neatly writing Lily's name on the top of a new folder.

"Let's talk about you," he says.

Lily does this blinking thing and looks up at me before she turns back to Hayden. "Um, okay?"

Hayden laughs and taps his pencil on the desk. "Do you have any ink already?"

"Oh! No. This will be my first."

"Ah. Very cool. So we're popping your ink cherry, then, yeah?"

Lily's cheeks turn pink, and she nods. "Uh, yeah, I guess."

"Do you have any ideas for designs?" he prompts.

"Oh! Yes! I found a few yesterday online." Lily pulls her phone out of her purse and scrolls through her pictures, showing Hayden a watercolor-looking heart. "I don't really want just a heart, but, like, I figured maybe we could take a pair of skates and set them inside the heart, you know, 'cause I'm a skater."

"Gotcha." Hayden flips through the images for a minute and

starts drawing right away, which is typically how it goes when we talk designs.

"Oh! But can we have one skate black and one white?" She tucks her hair behind her ears, exposing her earrings. "Like these?"

Hayden glances up and then leans in so he can check out the earrings. "Those are cool."

"Randy got them for me for Valentine's Day." And she's back to blushing.

Hayden spends a little more time asking questions, getting a feel for Lily's favorite colors and the designs she seems to like.

Once they're finished, he looks to me. "If you want, we can review the preliminary sketches for the team tattoos. Chris came in this morning to work on them a bit, and Jamie's probably here by now, too, so we can look them over, and you can tell us what you think and if we're on the right track."

"Definitely."

Hayden steps out, giving us a few minutes of privacy while he gets the other artists and the first-round sketches.

"So, what do you think, luscious?"

"You're right about him being intense, but he's nice."

"I don't mean Hayden. I mean the art."

"Oh." She shakes her head. "I'm excited to see what he does with the ideas, and I think your sleeve is going to be super sexy."

"Oh yeah?"

She nods. I don't have a chance to ask more questions because Chris, Hayden, and Jamie come in armed with folders. Lily stays for the first few minutes, but after a while Lisa pops her head in and asks if she wants to hang out with her while we talk details and business. Lily kisses me on the cheek and jumps up, leaving us to it.

It's another good half hour before we come out of the private room. Lily and Lisa are sitting behind the jewelry counter with a laptop and Hayden's custom album spread out in front of them, discussing their favorite tattoos. Hayden crosses over to his station and drops down in his chair, opening a drawer where he files his folders. The door tinkles, and a petite, curvy brunette holding a cupcake comes into the shop. It's not a real cupcake, but some kind of Tupperware deal that looks like a giant pink plastic cupcake.

Lisa hops off her stool and comes out from behind the jewelry display to hug her. I catch a glimpse of the back of the girl's shirt—or what there is to the back. It's tied behind the neck and one thin band cuts across the middle—and that's it, allowing most of her tattoo to be displayed. It's a set of wings that look incredibly familiar. It's definitely Hayden's work.

Hayden leans back in his chair. The ball of his tongue ring pops out and slides between his lips as he gives her a once-over. "Hey, kitten, perfect timing. Did you bring me some treats?"

She holds the cupcake container close to her chest, as if she expects him to try to steal it from her, and stays close to the jewelry counter. "They're for sharing."

"That's my least favorite word in the world." He inclines his chin, encouraging her to come closer. "Did you leave some at home?"

"What do you think?"

Lisa peeks inside the container, which apparently contains some kind of snack—maybe cupcakes like the shape implies—and snickers.

He beckons her closer. "Why don't you bring them over here and let me see?"

When she's within reach, he cranes to see in to the container.

She puts a hand out, warding him off. "Can you exert some self-control for a few seconds?" She gives Hayden a meaningful

35

look, her eyes darting my way for a moment.

"Oh, right. Sorry, kitten. Randy, this is my girlfriend, Tenley." He puts a hand on her waist.

Well, that explains the nickname.

"Hey. Hi!" Turning to me, she holds out a hand and shakes mine enthusiastically. "It's so nice to meet you. I made cupcakes. Would you like one before Hayden tries to tackle me for them?"

Hayden lifts an eyebrow. "I'm not that bad."

Lisa barks out a laugh, and Tenley snorts. She gives him her back while she opens the container, then takes two exaggerated steps away and offers me a cupcake. I'm more of a savory snack kind of guy, but these look incredible, so I take one.

"Did you make these?" I ask Tenley.

"I did."

"They look awesome." They're decorated with our team colors. I wonder if it was on purpose.

"Thanks." She gives me a huge smile.

Hayden watches her while she traipses over to the jewelry counter, introduces herself to Lily, and offers her and Lisa a cupcake. Chris, who disappeared a while ago, comes out of the back room and grabs one, too, making a big deal out of the black cupcake papers and the red and white decorations. Tenley flushes and gives him a look, like maybe she's embarrassed. Hayden crosses his arms over his chest and clears his throat.

Leaning on the counter, Tenley lifts a cupcake out of the container while watching him. Then she starts peeling off the wrapper, slowly. I feel like I'm watching some kind of weird foreplay, like cupcake-wrapper porn. It's almost as bad as the way Charlene and Darren are with each other lately.

"Keep pushing if you want to see where it gets you later, kitten," Hayden says.

Lily shoots me a look, but I have no idea what it means. I'm kind of entertained right now.

Tenley blinks at him. "Oh, did you want one?"

Hayden unfurls slowly from his chair, his expression dark. He stalks over to Tenley, who lifts the unwrapped cupcake to her mouth. Before she can take a bite, Hayden grabs her wrist. "I want this one."

"It's mine!"

"Not any more." He takes a massive bite, narrowly missing her fingers.

Tenley shrieks and laughs. "Oh my God! You're ridiculous!"

Hayden chews a few times and swallows, then swipes at his mouth with the back of his hand. He looks around, as if realizing there are other people witnessing this display.

He aims his grin at me. "I fucking love cupcakes."

"Especially Tee's," Chris says, his eyebrows wagging.

"Only Tenley's." He leans in and whispers something to her.

Lily's eyes go even wider, her mouth hanging open, her own cupcake still poised for biting. Lisa leans over and whispers something to her. She giggles and glances my way as she takes a bite of the cupcake and moans. "Oh my God, this is delicious."

"Right?" Hayden grabs another one from the container before Tenley can stop him. "I'll have some drawings for you when the guys come in to talk about their designs. Sound good?" he asks Lily.

"That sounds great!"

"Oh! Is Hayden going to design a tattoo for you?" Tenley asks.

"He is."

"He's a fantastic artist, and I'm not just saying that because I live with him." Tenley winks.

"Hayden did Tenley's back piece." Lisa motions for her to turn around.

Tenley shows Lily her back, and there's much *ooh*ing and *ahh*ing as Lily asks about the meaning and how painful it was while she gorges on cupcakes. I love how effortlessly she fits into all the pieces of my life.

On the way home, Lily's quiet, fingers drifting over my ink. "Everything okay, luscious?"

"Huh?" She glances at me. "Oh, yeah. Everything's great. Thanks for letting me tag along today. I had fun."

"You excited about the designs Hayden came up with?"

She nods enthusiastically. "Oh yeah. Definitely. His girlfriend's tattoo is insane. I can't believe the detail on that. I can't even imagine how long something like that would take."

"A lot of hours, that's for sure." My sleeve took about twenty hours, and while Tenley is petite, it's a lot of skin to cover.

"It's a gorgeous tattoo."

"It is," I agree.

"Do you think it's sexy?" She glances at the flower decorating my hand.

"A full back tattoo? Or Tenley's specifically?"

Lily shrugs. "I don't know. Either? Both?"

"Sure. I guess. Do *you* think it's sexy?"

She nods. "Those two have insane chemistry."

"Yeah."

"That cupcake thing was intense. I was worried there was going to be a throw down." Lily laughs, but it's a little breathy.

I slip a hand under her hair and run my thumb down the ridges of her spine. "I bet he can't give her orgasms just by looking at her."

Lily snorts. "Neither can you."

"Pretty damn close."

"Mmm." She taps her lip. "Maybe I should get Hayden to design something bigger."

"One step at time, luscious. Starting small is probably a good plan."

"But if that goes well, I could get something more detailed."

"If that's what you want." I try to keep my grin contained. I think I may have created a monster, and I'm not even a little bit sorry about that.

4

HAIR BRAIDING

CHRIS

Once Hayden finishes the consults with Randy and his girlfriend—who makes Lisa look voluptuous—we show him the options for the various tattoos he and his teammates will be getting later in the summer.

After they leave, I don't have another appointment scheduled until two in the afternoon, so I figure I can run across the street to see Sarah—the girl I've been hanging out with for the past several months.

It's not serious. At least that's how I'm spinning it right now. Mostly we see each other when we can. Since she's a full-time grad student with a waitressing gig on the side, and I work weird hours as a tattoo artist, even the convenience of her living across the street from my work is often hard to take advantage of. But not today. She's home, based on the text I just received, and looking forward to a visit. Which I'm hoping will include an orgasm—maybe more than one for Sarah, if I'm on my game this afternoon.

I use the key to get in the back door and take the stairs at a jog. I have more than an hour before I have to be back. Maybe we can even squeeze in lunch or something—if we have time.

I don't bother knocking since Sarah knows I'm on my way over. I open the door to find the living room empty. "Sarah?"

She comes rushing down the hall from the direction of her bedroom, looking frazzled. I take in her attire. Actually, I take in the entire package. She's wearing one of my oversized shirts and running a brush through her long, pale blond hair.

She tosses the brush on the table, but misses, so it drops to the floor.

"Hey! Hi!" Sarah launches herself at me, throwing her arms around my neck, hugging me tightly. The enthusiastic affection is short lived, and she backs up. "How much time do you have?"

"I don't have to be back at the shop until ten to two."

She glances at the clock on the stove, and her eyes light up. "That's more than ninety whole minutes! What should we do?"

"Hmm." I tap my lip. "Maybe I can braid your hair, and we can talk about our life goals."

Sarah wrinkles her nose. "Or maybe you can check to see whether I'm wearing panties or not."

"So hair braiding is out?"

"Uh, yeah, unless it's a euphemism for taking your clothes off." She grabs my hand and pulls me toward her bedroom.

"What if I just want to talk?"

"You can do that naked."

"Don't you want to know how my morning was?" I ask as she pulls me through the doorway and into her pretty, feminine bedroom. The sheets are still rumpled, despite it being after noon. Sarah works late hours, and it's Saturday, so she doesn't have classes to contend with today.

Turning, she pushes up on her toes to kiss my jaw. "How was

41

your morning?"

Sarah's a tall girl. She's long and willowy, and she probably could've been a model. The career she's choosing has better longevity, though. An MBA will go a lot further for a lot longer. And once she's done, her side job serving drinks at a strip club will be history. I'm the only person she takes her clothes off for, though. Thank fuck.

"One of the professional hockey players we do work for came in for a consult." This is actually something I'm pretty excited about, although I'm not sure Sarah gives much of a shit about hockey.

Sarah slides her hands under my shirt, her nails running over my abs. "Seriously? Back for more?"

"Yeah."

She stops her quest to get my shirt off, her palms flat on my chest. "Holy crap. That's really cool. Which player? Was it Waters again?"

"Ballistic was in today, but a bunch of the guys from the team are coming in at the end of summer, and they're all getting work done."

"That's amazing." She edges her hand up a little more. "That's kind of like having celebrities in the shop, right?"

"Kind of."

"I'm glad things are going so well. You deserve something good right now." She's sincere, even though she's still working on getting my shirt off—and she's not just talking about sex.

The past few months have been challenging for personal reasons, so good things haven't been all that easy to come by. Sarah's one of those rare good things, and since I don't get to see her all that often, I choose not to fill our time with depressing talk.

"You got anything else good you wanna give me?" I slip a

finger in to the waistband of her shorts, pulling them out so I can check to see if she's lying about the lack of panties. I get a glimpse of white cotton. They're my fucking favorite. "Playing tricks on me with these, huh?" I edge a finger under the elastic.

"Keeping you on your toes." She gives my shirt another tug, and this time I help with getting it over my head. Sarah sighs and smooths her hands over my shoulders and down my biceps, her eyes tracking the movement on my right arm—the one with the full sleeve. Then she continues over my chest until she reaches the waist of my jeans, popping the button.

We take our time, which is a luxury. Mostly we get middle-of-the-night sessions or quickies between tightly scheduled clients. When I'm done loving on her body, she rests her cheek on my chest.

"I can hear your heart," she whispers.

"What's it saying?" I smooth my hand over her hair.

"The same thing over and over. I think it's trying to put me to sleep." She pushes up on an elbow, her lids heavy. "When are you going to design a tattoo for me?"

It's a question she's asked before, more than once. I keep putting her off—not because I don't want to put art on her, but because I do. The temptation to make myself permanent in her life in some way is hard to resist.

"When I get more than two hours at a time with you."

Sarah kisses my chin. "My internship isn't far off, and once it's over I should have loads of time, relatively speaking."

"I guess you better figure out what you want then, 'cause I'm booked up until halfway through the summer already." I try not to think about what's going to happen to this thing we have when her internship is finished and her job prospects open up.

"You don't think you can fit me in somewhere between now and then?"

"You think you get special privileges or something?"

She bites my shoulder. "I better get special privileges."

I check the clock on her nightstand and change the subject. "I still got another half hour. You want me to braid your hair now?"

Sarah throws her leg over my hip. "I can think of way better ways to spend all that time."

I let her pull me on top of her again, and then I distract her from conversations about body art with my hands and mouth.

5

WE NEED IN ON THAT

VIOLET

Alex, my extraordinarily awesome, professional-hockey-playing husband, left at some god-awful hour this morning to hit the green with the guys. Apparently golf is an all-day event, so we're having a girls' afternoon. It's not super hot out, but it's sunny, and Alex cranked up the heat in the pool. Plus we have those outdoor heater things stationed around us to make it feel like July even though it's not even close.

"I don't understand the purpose of golf," I muse aloud.

"It's like every other sport with sticks and balls. You aim for a hole, and if you get it in, you score." Charlene flips onto her stomach and unties the top of her bikini so she can avoid lines. If she were alone—or at Darren's—she'd probably go without a top.

"Sounds like you're talking about sex, not golf," Lily snickers. She's on her third drink, so she's nice and loopy.

"You think everything is about sex thanks to Horny Nut Sac," I shoot back. It's my favorite nickname for Randy, her boyfriend and Alex's teammate.

"I think all sports with balls and sticks are a lot the same, aren't they?" Sunny says from under the shade of her umbrella. She's rocking a pretty sweet baby belly since my brother, Buck, who everyone else has taken to calling Miller since that happens to be his real name, knocked her up. She only has a few months to go before she pops the cork on this one.

I consider the similarities, particularly between golf and hockey. "I guess golf is kind of like playing hockey, except with smaller sticks, and balls instead of pucks, and grass instead of ice, and a tiny hole instead of a gaping one."

Lily chokes on her drink and ends up spit-spraying it all over herself. "No one likes gaping holes!"

Charlene snickers along with her, but Sunny purses her lips. "Maybe you should have water after that one."

"You're probably right," Lily agrees.

"It just seems boring. I've never seen anyone fight on a green." I tip my bottle back and drain the last of my drink.

"Once Miller put Randy in a headlock for sending him into the weeds," Lily says. "But that's the best I've got."

"Yeah. Like I said, boring. And what's with the plaid requirement?" I ask.

"Darren looks good in plaid," Charlene says.

"Personally I think Randy looks hot in one of those golf shirts and plaid shorts, especially with the sleeve..." Lily trails off.

"Do you need a minute alone?" I grin evilly. "Oh wait, you don't actually need physical contact to have an orgasm, so you can just daydream your way to one and we won't even know unless you get all moany."

Lily lifts her sunglasses and quirks a brow. "At what point does the laundry room orgasm stop being a source of entertainment for you?"

Last Christmastime Randy locked Lily in our laundry room. In the three minutes they were alone, he managed to give her an orgasm—fully dressed. How do I know this? We busted down the door and witnessed the voodoo magic.

"Seriously, though, Lily, I need to know how you do that," Charlene says.

"Do what?"

"Have spontaneous orgasms." Charlene props herself up on her elbows and we all get a look at her boobs before she realizes she's showing us her nipples. Her *pierced* nipples.

"When the hell did you get your nipples pierced?" I ask.

Apparently I'm rather loud about it, because she throws the closest thing at me, which happens to be Andy's ball. He jumps up and bounds after it when it ricochets off my chair and lands in the pool.

Charlene looks down and back up. "A while ago."

"And you didn't tell me? Is Darren into that?" Sometimes I wonder about those two.

Her grin is all smirky. "It's not like body piercing is something I'm just going to drop into conversation. And yes, Darren likes them."

Lily perks right up. "Did it hurt?"

"The clamp is a little uncomfortable, but otherwise it wasn't too bad."

Lily frowns. "Clamp?"

"They use a clamp to pinch the skin before they feed the needle through."

Lily puts her hand over her modestly sized boobs. I'm not saying that to be mean. She has little boobs, just like the rest of her.

"Doesn't that hurt?" she asks.

Charlene shrugs. "I have a pretty high pain tolerance, so I

47

didn't find it too bad."

"I wonder if Alex would lose his shit over something like this." I move from my chair to the patio and sit in front of Charlene. "Sit up. I want to check those out."

"What?"

"Sit up and show me your nipples."

Charlene rolls her eyes, but she complies. We've been friends for a very long time. She trussed me up in weird fetish gear with all the leather and chains very recently when I got hitched in Vegas, so she can sure as hell show me her blinged-out nips.

She gets into a cross-legged position to match mine, and I lean in until I'm only a few inches away from her boobs. Charlene has nice boobs. They're a lot smaller than mine, but bigger than Lily's. And her nipples are also more nipply than mine.

"Can I look, too?" Lily asks.

"Might as well while they're hanging out," Charlene replies.

Lily sets down her drink and weaves her way over to us. Even half-wasted she's way more graceful than I am.

She plunks herself down beside me, and we stare at Charlene's boobs. "Wow. So it doesn't hurt that much?"

"Like I said, I have a high pain tolerance."

Lily keeps up with the questions. "Are they super sensitive afterward?"

"Well, yeah, but that's the point."

Sunny cups her boobs protectively. "My boobs are so sensitive these days, I can't even imagine."

"Yeah. I definitely wouldn't recommend you get your nipples pierced right now." Charlene says.

Sunny shakes her head. "I don't really like pain. And I can't wear earrings that aren't solid gold because my skin reacts."

"They can use titanium." Charlene flicks her nipple. "That's what I have."

Lily slaps her muscular, super-thin thigh that doesn't ever jiggle. "You know what, I went with Randy to see his tattoo artist yesterday, and they have a piercer there."

"Ooooh! I think Alex gets his tattoos at the same place. What's it called?" I ask.

"Inked Armor. Does Alex see Hayden?" Lily does that thing with her hands that's normally reserved for when she talks about being excited to see Randy, which really means getting naked and being on the receiving end of seven million consecutive orgasms.

"Uh, no. Alex's artist is Chris. He's a blond guy, looks like he should be in one of those military Xbox games? Last time I was there I didn't really pay much attention beyond the fact that they're hot, and I could never get a tattoo because I worry I'd end up with something awful forever. Like that girl who let her boyfriend tattoo his name on her face."

"Someone actually did that?" Sunny looks appropriately mortified.

"Horrible, right? It's stuff like that that makes me seem sane and mostly normal." I'll never understand why people do such crazy things to their bodies. Although now I'm considering what Alex would think of nipple piercings. He liked it when I blinged out my beaver, maybe he'd be into blinged-out boobs, too.

"Can I lie back down now?" Charlene asks.

"Yeah. Go ahead." I get up and go back to my chair, but Lily stays where she is.

"So, I don't know if you all know this, but all the guys are going to get tattoos together at the end of the summer," she announces, her eyes still on Charlene. "I think we should all go, too."

"I remember Darren saying something about that," Charlene muses, and Sunny nods her agreement.

"I'm not getting a tattoo," Sunny says.

"I don't mean to get a tattoo. Well, I'm getting one—"

"You're getting a tattoo?" Sunny's voice is all squeaky.

Lily nods. "Yeah. Randy's artist, Hayden, is drawing something up. Sweet Lord, that man is intense, and seriously hot."

"All the guys in there are," I say.

"Right?" Lily fans her face. "Hayden's all angsty and broody, and he's got two full sleeves. He looks like a model. And the other guys, they're just as hot. Honestly, I was never big into tattoos before Randy, but now..."

"Are there pictures of these guys?" Charlene interrupts.

"I don't know. Maybe? Let me check." Lily pops up and runs across the patio to get her phone. She punches a bunch of buttons and frowns while she scrolls. "A lot of the images are sample designs and custom pieces... Oh! Wait—this is Hayden!"

She flips the phone around and shows Sunny the picture before she shows us.

Now, I'm not really a full-sleeve tattoo kind of girl, but I get Lily's appreciation for Randy's body art, because he's a nice-looking guy with a nice arm and cool designs on it. I check out the picture on Lily's phone. I'm pretty sure the hottie taking up her screen is the guy I got a brief glimpse of before Chris took Alex and me into the private room the one time I was there. From what I recall, and can confirm from this tiny little phone picture, he's a panty incinerator.

Charlene grabs the phone to get a closer look. "He can't really be that hot in real life."

"Oh, he's even hotter. Seriously, doesn't he look like he should be on the cover of magazines?" Lily says.

"Or inside them naked?" Charlene adds.

"I think Miller is better looking than that guy," Sunny says.

"Yeah, but you have an unusual affinity for yetis, so that's not really a surprise." Buck is blond, like Sunny, so all the hair on his arms and legs mostly blends in. There's still a lot of it, but he trims routinely. When I was a teenager I used to come into the bathroom to find body hair tumbleweeds all over the place. It was gross.

"You have to admit this guy is hot, though." Lily points to her phone. "You just need to meet him. I can't explain it. He's intense. Like, more intense than Randy, if that's even possible."

"Did you act like this when you were there with Randy?"

"Act like what?"

"Like you're about to have heart palpitations and a case of the vapors." Not that I blame her. I mean, the guy is smoking, even if he is kind of wiry. He reminds me of the emo guys in high school that I used to be a little afraid of. But not actually afraid, more like I was never going to be cool enough to hang out with them.

Charlene nabs the phone again. "You know, if this guy had a beard, he'd look a lot like Randy."

Lily leans over her shoulder. "You know, I kind of thought the same thing. I've never seen Randy without the beard."

"Ohhh, maybe you should ask him to shave it, just for comparison sake," I suggest.

"I'm not sure he'd go for that, or that I want him to. I kind of love his beard." Lily sigh-shudders.

"Don't you find it scratchy? I always find Alex's beard scratchy during playoffs. Sometimes it chafes my beaver, and I have to put aloe on it."

"I'm sure Sunny really wanted to know that," Charlene mutters.

I'm not sure Sunny is even paying attention since she's busy looking at her own phone, but I apologize anyway.

Sunny shrugs. "I always find there's less chafing after the first two weeks. Sometimes we take a day in between cookie-eating sessions until he reaches the soft and not scratchy stage."

"Well, Randy's beard is super soft. He conditions it a lot, though."

"With your vagina!" I say.

Lily snickers, and we fist bump.

By the time the guys get back from golfing, it's time for dinner, and we're all sun baked and hammered—except for Sunny, who's the only one smart enough to keep reapplying sunscreen throughout the day. It was a sunny, and we forgot to account for the fact that we've been hiding under warm clothes for several months, except for the few days we spent getting me hitched in Vegas.

After dinner, everyone goes home, and I take a cool shower to help ease the heat on my over-sunned skin. Apparently my time honeymooning in Hawaii didn't provide enough of a base to avoid a burn. I grab the aloe lotion and drop down on the bed beside Alex, groaning my displeasure at the sandpaper feel of the comforter.

"You look a little overcooked. Want me to put that on your back?" Alex nods to the bottle in my hand.

I pass it over. "That'd be awesome."

He pulls my shirt over my head and makes a disapproving sound. "Did you wear sunscreen at all?"

"I forgot to reapply."

"Clearly." He drops a small kiss on my shoulder, then reaches around and cups my boobs in his palms, sighing. "At least these aren't burned."

My nipples are each framed with a pasty white triangle. "I imagine burned nipples aren't very pleasant."

Alex makes a sound of agreement as he circles one with his

finger. He keeps doing that until it's perfectly hard. Then he does it some more.

"What do you think of nipple rings?"

His finger stills. "What?"

"Pierced nipples. How do you feel about them?"

"You mean how would I feel about having my nipples pierced?"

"No. How would you feel about me having mine pierced?"

He puts a protective palm over my nipple, as if he's shielding it from our conversation. "Uhhh…I don't really know. It's not something I've ever thought about."

"So you've never been with someone who had nipple piercings?"

"No. Why the sudden interest in putting extra holes in your sensitive parts?"

I shrug. "I don't know. Charlene has hers pierced."

"So you think you need to have yours done to match?"

"No. I was just curious. You liked it when I bedazzled my beaver; I wondered if you'd like my boobs bedazzled, too."

Alex checks out my naked, unbedazzled beaver. "That was so fucking hot."

"I can do it again if you want."

"Yeah?"

"Definitely."

"I'll be a little more careful so they last longer…whenever you decide you want to decorate your pretty pussy."

I shiver—not because I'm succumbing to heat stroke, but because of his pussy reference. "I'll make an appointment next week."

"Or I could set up a spa day for you."

"You don't need to do that."

"You've been working really hard lately; you deserve a day

of pampering."

As much as I've tried not to succumb to it, I kind of love being doted on by Alex. "You're so good to me."

"I try, baby." He holds up the aloe lotion. "Why don't you roll over, and I'll rub this all over your sexy, naked body."

"And then you'll rub Super MC all over my sexy, naked beaver?"

"You read my mind."

6

STEEL

DARREN

I check my email while I wait for Waters. His most recent text, which came two minutes ago, tells me he's running a little behind. This isn't abnormal, even if it's Saturday. Particularly since he got married.

I don't think it's Violet's fault, though. Of the two of them, she's way more prompt than he is.

Another message comes in while I'm email scrolling. It's from Charlene, the woman I've been seeing for the past year. It's a pretty casual thing. Sort of. We have fun together, and we're into the same things, so it works out well. Most of the time, anyway. Things got a little tense when Alex and Violet got married a few weeks ago, but they've settled down since we got back from Vegas, so we're status quo again.

I flip to my messages. The one from Charlene is brief and to the point.

Busy 2nite?

I hate text speak. She knows this. Also, this is Charlene's way of asking if I'm available. My reply is far more direct.

> Do you want to see me?

The dots appear, telling me she's composing her response. They stop for a second, then start again. Then stop again before a message appears.

> Yes

I type a reply. It's not a question.

> Dinner at 7

Her reply is much faster this time.

> What shld I wear?

Charlene is more than capable of choosing her own outfits, but if she's asking, it means she wants me to pick for her. I consider that for a moment, mentally filtering through her wardrobe, both dresses and lingerie.

> Do you have time to
> get something new?

She sends one back right away.

> Yes. Any color pref?

I tap my lip, pondering some more.

> Purple dress. Lavender lingerie.
> Use the card I gave you.

The next message doesn't come for several minutes. This time there are images accompanying the message with possible screenshot lingerie options.

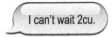

I can't wait 2cu.

I flip through the pictures she's sent: the first is sweet, the second is sexy, the third is slutty. Charlene likes to keep things interesting in the bedroom. Frankly, so do I.

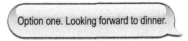

Option one. Looking forward to dinner.

There's a tap on the trunk, and I look in the rearview mirror to find Alex waiting for me to pop it. When I do, he tosses his bag inside, closes the trunk, and comes around to the passenger side.

He drops into the seat, grinning. "Hey, man, sorry I'm late."

"No you're not." I shift the car into gear and pull into traffic, heading for the gym.

"You're right. I'm not." He adjusts his seat—Charlene was the last one to sit there, so his knees are currently hitting the dash. "Why does Charlene sit so far forward?"

I shrug, because answering that will tell him far more than he needs to know about what happened the last time she and I went for a drive. "You have an actual excuse for being late, or you just couldn't get your lazy ass out of bed?"

"I surprised Violet with a spa day." That grin of his widens even more.

"What does that have to do with you being late?"

"She wanted to thank me in advance for being so thoughtful."

"Over a spa day? Don't the girls go all the time?" Charlene's nails are always perfectly manicured, and I know she's not doing them herself.

"Dude, do you have any idea how relaxed and happy Violet is after a day at the spa? And smooth. Every single inch of skin is like satin. And she smells fucking fantastic." He shifts around in his seat, his knee bouncing with excitement.

"So you're sending her for your own benefit?"

Alex gives me a look, like I'm dumb. "It's mutually beneficial. She gets to relax for the day, and when she comes home, I get to enjoy the aftermath of her relaxation. Usually for several hours."

I tap the steering wheel, considering this. "But can't she set that up on her own?"

"Well, of course she can, but it makes me look good when I'm the one who does it for her. All I have to do is call and ask them for the deluxe spa day package, and they do the rest. Then I reap the benefits when she gets home. It's win all around."

"I wonder if Charlene would want to go with her."

"Probably. I made the appointment early this week, but sometimes they have cancellations. You want me to call and find out if they have space?"

"Sure."

Alex makes the call while I drive to the gym. He's put on hold while they check for openings. A few seconds later, I learn it's my lucky day because someone had to cancel on short notice. He's still on the phone when I pull into the underground lot. I should probably check to make sure Charlene is available for whatever Alex is helping me set up.

I call instead of text, because it's easier. She answers on the second ring, sounding out of breath.

"Hi, sexy. Did I catch you at a bad time?"

"No. Nope. Not at all. What's up?"

"I'd like to make a change in your plans for today." I glance at Alex who's giving me a strange look.

"Oh? You don't have to cancel, do you?"

I like how concerned she sounds about the prospect. "No. Nothing like that. Violet's going to the spa today. Would you like to join her?"

"At the spa?"

"Yes. At the spa."

"Umm...that sounds nice, but I don't have an appointment, and the place she goes is usually booked up weeks out."

"I've already taken care of that, but only if you're interested. Otherwise I can cancel."

"Wait. What?" She sounds confused.

"The appointment is already made if you'd like to go. I believe there are several services you can take advantage of."

"Seriously?"

I'm not sure whether I should be entertained by her disbelief or not. "Yes. Seriously."

"That would be amazing."

Now it's my turn to smile, although she can't see it. I give Alex the thumbs-up, and he finalizes the appointments and writes the start and end times on a piece of paper so I can tell Charlene.

"Excellent," I tell her. "I'll take care of everything. All you have to do is show up. You can coordinate with Violet on getting there, and your first appointment is at ten thirty. Your final appointment will end at four. Of course, if there's anything you want to do differently, feel free to make changes."

"Okay. Um, Darren?"

"Yeah, sexy?"

"This sounds wonderful, but I might not have time to go dress and lingerie shopping." Her voice is soft, nervous and excited.

"Hmm... You have a point. Would you still like to try to make time for that, or should I expect that you'll be unable to fulfill that request?"

"Would you still like me to try to make time for that?"

I don't answer right away. If Charlene is worried about dress shopping, she's not going to be nearly as relaxed—in fact she'll be on edge, which usually isn't a bad thing. But I feel like it might defeat the purpose of what I'm trying to do here.

"I don't think that's necessary. Of course, if you have the time, please feel free to use it, but it would be perfectly acceptable for you to provide options for me to choose from when I pick you up. Does that seem like a reasonable compromise?"

"It sounds perfectly reasonable, Darren."

"Fantastic. Enjoy your day, and I'll see you tonight." I hang up the phone feeling good about myself, at least until I get a load of the look on Alex's face. "What?"

"What the shit was that about?"

"What was what about?"

He shakes his head. "I don't know about you sometimes, man." He puts his phone to his ear. After a moment he says, "Hey, baby, I've got another surprise for you." There's a pause while he listens to whatever Violet is saying. Then he laughs. "No, baby, not that kind of surprise. Yeah. You can pick some of those up—not the ones covered in sugar though. They're messy, and I don't like the way they feel. Yeah—Yeah. Those are my favorite, but that's not why I'm calling... Listen, Charlene's gonna spend the day with you at the spa."

There's some high-pitched shrieking, and Alex laughs again.

"Darren set it up for her on my suggestion, so feel free to come up with some creative ways to thank me later, if you want." He's quiet for several seconds, his grin growing wider. Eventually he ends the call and shoves his phone in his pocket. "Tonight's gonna be fucking awesome."

"Agreed."

We get out of the car and take the elevator up to the gym.

"You can't use your sex-a-thon tonight as an excuse to pussy out on today's workout," I warn him.

He flips me the bird. "Whatever, dude. This is my warm-up."

We start with laps on the indoor track and move to weights. Alex is still recovering from his accident last season, so he's on low weight and high reps for his shoulder. He gets frustrated pretty easily with how slow his progress is, but I don't let him push himself beyond what's reasonable. We've been friends long enough that he doesn't get too pissed when I tell him to take it easy.

It's harder for him to stay within his limits when we're working out with the team, so he and I go at least three times a week on our own—and that's on top of his physical therapy sessions.

After weights, we hit the pool and then the hot tub, followed by the sauna. No one's in there but us, so we sit down and relax, letting the heat do its job.

"I can't wait to check out the tattoo designs." Alex runs his palm over the most recent addition to his body art—he had The Cup tattooed on the inside of his right bicep after we won it. He doesn't have a ton of ink, but he keeps adding to it, so I'm assuming at some point he might end up making it a half sleeve if nothing else.

If there's one thing I know about addictions, it's that once you get a taste of something you like, it's hard not to keep going back for more. I don't think it's any different with body art. Ballistic is about to start another full sleeve, and Romero has a massive back piece. Miller and I are the only ones who haven't bitten the ink bullet before now. I figure if there's one thing I can safely put permanently on my skin, it's something hockey-related.

"We go in to see them soon, right?"

"Yeah. Ballistic says they look amazing, but that's not really a surprise."

I nod. I've been to Inked Armor once for the original consult on the team tattoo, just after the season ended. Since I started seeing Charlene, I've spent a lot more time hanging out with the other guys on my team who have girlfriends. It's not something I usually do, considering my relationships with women haven't ever been all that conventional. Until Charlene. And it's still not exactly conventional.

Alex rolls his shoulder. I have a feeling he pushed it a little too hard today, despite my efforts to rein him in. He's competitive, and he has a hard time with the idea that he might not be in top form by the time training camp starts.

"Can I ask you something?" he says.

"Yeah, man, shoot." I'm stretched out on the sauna bench, head back, eyes closed.

"It's about Charlene."

I try not to flinch, or react in any way. Alex and I are tight, almost like brothers, but we don't get into deep discussions about my relationship with Charlene. She's his wife's best friend, and giving him too many personal details when it comes to her is complicated. It's not that I don't trust him, because I do. But since he's married, I figure whatever I tell him I'm also telling Violet. So I pretty much avoid the topic.

"Violet says she has her nipples pierced."

I crack a lid. He's not looking at me; he's staring at the ceiling.

"What's Violet doing looking at Charlene's nipples?"

"So she does?"

"Yeah." I have to work hard not to picture Charlene's nipples in my head, or the conversation that led to her getting her nipples pierced. Or how fucking hot it is when she wears the delicate gold chain that connects them to each other, or the one that hooks to her belly ring. She looks so pretty and soft with her clothes on, but the second they come off and the lights are dimmed, she's a whole different woman. I fucking love it. Most of the time.

"What's that like?"

"What are Charlene's nipples like?"

"Violet asked me how I felt about her getting her nipples pierced, and honestly, I have no fucking clue because it's not something I've ever thought about. But apparently it's something she's considering, so I figure I should be informed by someone who knows the deal."

I squeeze the back of my neck, working out how I want to word this. "Well, Charlene likes them because they make sensation much more intense."

"So it's good?"

"Yeah."

"Like, orgasm good?"

"For Charlene, yeah."

"And you like them?"

"I think they're sexy on the right woman." And Charlene is exactly the right woman. The two-month healing time was the best foreplay ever.

Alex nods thoughtfully and doesn't ask any more questions. I don't give him any more answers.

After four hours at the gym—half of it spent not working out—I make a stop at one of the stores where Charlene likes to shop, based on the purchases that appear on the credit card I gave her. She doesn't abuse it, which is why she has it. She only uses it when I request that she get something new, or sexy.

I'm well aware that her salary and mine don't come close to matching, so I don't think it's fair that she has to spend her own money on something I'm going to appreciate for only a few minutes before I peel it off her incredibly sexy, toned body.

I head straight for one of the salesladies and tell her exactly what I'm looking for. Apparently, dark purple is not popular this time of year, and the only thing they have has a floral print on it. Charlene prefers solid colors to prints, so I browse the store, looking for something I think would look good on her curvy, lithe frame. I end up buying two dresses, because I like them both equally, and I'm also partial to giving Charlene options.

My next stop is the lingerie store. I spend much more time there. Charlene and I have very different taste in her lingerie. Not that I mind the things she picks—they're interesting. But I prefer slightly more refined options. I'm willing to compromise, sometimes. Not tonight, however.

I find exactly the right thing, and a few others she might like as well, and I have the saleslady take the tags off before she wraps them in tissue paper.

"Are you sure you don't want to leave the tags? In case she needs a different size?"

"I'm positive I know exactly what size she wears." I tap my credit card on the counter.

"Of course." She gives me a conspiratorial wink.

I smile, but I don't understand what the wink is about. I can't imagine not being aware of what size the woman I get into bed with on a regular basis wears. I also don't want Charlene to see the price tags on this stuff; otherwise she's liable to think she needs to make it up to me in some way. We have enough of a power struggle as it is. I don't need to make it worse with what's supposed to be a gift.

The cashier rings it up to the tune of nine hundred dollars, which I'll gladly pay, because Charlene in pretty things is a sight to behold.

I head home, shower again—because the ones at the gym don't make me feel particularly clean—shave, and hit my closet.

As I rifle through my clothes, I shoot Charlene a message asking about her day at the spa. She sends me a picture of her lavender-painted toe and fingernails.

Instead of messaging her again, I call. She answers on the second ring.

"Having fun with Violet?" I ask.

"So much. Thank you again for this."

"No thanks necessary. What time do you think you'll be home?"

"Violet's just finishing her last treatment, so we'll be leaving here in the next half hour."

I check the time. It's four thirty, which gives me and Charlene plenty of time.

"I assume you won't be able to go shopping."

"It's unlikely. Is that going to be a problem?"

"I anticipated that might happen, so no, it's not a problem." I finger a dark gray tie with fine purple stripes and wait for her response.

"Oh. Okay." As expected, she's not pleased by this.

"I have a request, though, if you feel the timing is adequate."

"Oh? What kind of request?" Excitement makes her voice waver.

"I went shopping for you."

"Really?"

I wish I could see her expression right now. I'm not sure if her surprise is a good thing. "Really."

"What did I do to deserve all this pampering?" she asks softly.

"You put up with me. Isn't that enough?"

Charlene laughs. "Like it's such a chore. So what's the request?"

"I'd like to come by your place a little early so you have time to get dressed."

"And you want me to model everything for you?"

"Mmm."

"How would you like me to answer the door?"

I close my eyes and filter through all of the ways Charlene has answered her door in the past, in various states of undress. "Not naked would be preferable."

"Well, that's no fun."

"I'll see you at six."

She sighs. "Okay."

"And Charlene?"

"Yes?"

"Don't forget your pearls."

"Of course not, Darren."

I arrive at Charlene's at 5:57. I chose the tie with purple stripes to match the dress and lingerie I've purchased, which is hanging from my finger. I ring the doorbell and hear the quick clip of shoes coming down the hall. She's wearing heels. I'm excited to find out what she's paired them with.

She opens the door a crack, enough for me to catch a glimpse of one hazel eye and her lip-glossed smile. "Hi."

I raise the bag dangling from my finger. "I come bearing gifts."

She steps back and opens the door just enough to let me in. There's a good reason for her to stay out of her neighbors' line of sight. Charlene isn't exactly naked, but she's close. She's wearing a pair of black heels and, of course, her pearls. The fine gold chain I love so much connects her pierced nipples. My dick is immediately annoyed that we don't have nearly enough time to play before we have to leave for dinner.

Anticipating a greeting such as this, I took care of myself before I left my place. It takes the edge off, but getting through dinner is probably going to be a challenge. I close the door and turn the lock—not that I expect anyone to come barging in, but Charlene is mostly naked, and I don't want anyone to see her in this particular state but me.

"Should we go upstairs so I can model everything for you?" She has her hands clasped behind her back. It pushes her breasts out and pulls on the delicate chain across her chest.

I follow the fine gold links with a fingertip. "I think down here is better, don't you?"

She shivers when I graze the swell of her breast and stop short of her nipple. "If that's what you'd prefer."

I give the chain a tug and her eyes flutter shut. Her lips part, and her breath leaves her on a tiny, almost inaudible whimper.

"Come with me." With my finger still hooked under the chain, I guide her down the hall. I have her wait at the entrance to the living room while I pull all the curtains closed. Then I move the coffee table out of the way and survey the room. I can feel Charlene watching me, but I don't look at her—mostly because if I do I'm liable to say fuck trying on the things I bought for her, and then the entire point is lost.

I sit down on the end of the couch and put the bag in the middle, intentionally making it impossible for her to sit beside me. "Why don't you come have a seat?"

Charlene looks a little disappointed, maybe because I've asked her to come to me rather than retrieving her. She keeps her hands clasped behind her back, the muscles in her legs flexing with each step. Her hair is pulled up, with loose tendrils framing her fine features. When she reaches the couch, she unclasps her hands and sits slowly at the very edge opposite me and the bag.

She doesn't cross her legs; instead she keeps her knees together, palms covering them.

I have to keep reminding myself that I have a plan for tonight, and I need to stick to it.

I stretch one arm across the back of the couch. "Go ahead and open it."

Charlene shifts a little closer and peeks inside the bag. She pulls out the first wrapped item. "How many things did you get for me?"

"A few."

She bites her lip, carefully peels off the sticker and unwraps the tissue paper. Inside is a pale, lacy bra and panty set. I wait for her reaction. This isn't something Charlene would choose on her own. Before I started adding pieces to her collection, everything was black, blood red, or dark purple—some of it with quite a bit of…embellishment. I don't have a problem with any of those colors, or the leather/metal enhancements. She looks amazing in everything she puts on her body, but I also like her in pretty, soft things, because they match far better who she is on the inside, even if she would like that to not be the case.

Charlene glances up at me, her brow arched. "This is pretty."

I grin. "I know."

"Should I try it on before I open the next one?"

"Open them all. Then you can try on the one you like the best first."

By the time she's finished unwrapping everything—it takes a long time since she's so methodical about it—it's already twenty after six.

I'm a little concerned at this point that Charlene isn't going to have enough time to try all the items on. I'm also worried about the current state of my dick. My balls are starting to ache from the hard-on I've had since she answered the door. I really don't want to have to sit through three hours of dinner, able to picture perfectly whatever she chooses to wear under her dress.

"Will you help me with this?" I'm unsurprised when Charlene picks up the lavender lace corset with dark purple ribbon accents. It has no cups, framing her breasts rather than covering them.

"Of course."

I wait while she loosens the ribbon lacing up the back. When it's ready, she stands in front of me and steps delicately into the corset, shimmying it up her legs and over her hips to her waist. Then she turns and gives me her back. Her ass—her perfect, luscious, sweet ass that I'm going to do dirty, unspeakable things to later—is right in my face. I run my hands over her hips, resisting the urge to cup and squeeze, which is probably what she wants me to do.

Instead, I move her forward a few steps until she's in the center of the throw rug. Across the room on the wall is a huge mirror, giving us an excellent view of her new lingerie. I carefully pull the ribbons, making sure it's even on either side before I move down to the next loop, until I'm at the dip in her spine. Then I help her roll on and fasten garters, stockings, and gloves, all with the same ribbon accents.

"What do you think?" she asks.

I glance up to meet her gaze in the mirror. She's fingering her pearls.

"I think I should call the restaurant and tell them we need a later reservation."

7

ADD ONS

ALEX

It's the middle of the week, and Violet is working on an account tonight, so I'm out with the guys, doing what we do when it's off-season and we're not working out: drinking beer and watching sports.

"They've got all the preliminary designs ready for us at Inked Armor. You guys wanna go check them out this weekend?" Randy's focused on his phone.

Lance leans in closer, and his brow furrows. "Is the one with the heart for you? Gonna get that tattooed on your ass cheek?"

Ballistic elbows him in the ribs, causing Lance to hunch over and bang into the table, almost knocking over my pint glass.

"Lily's having a design made up, you dick."

"Lily's getting a tattoo?" Lily's always been pretty straight-laced and not the type I'd imagine would be interested in body art—but clearly I'm wrong, or dating Ballistic has changed that.

Randy smiles. "She sure is. I'm rubbing off on her."

The way his eyes light up tells me he means this literally and figuratively. Lily's my little sister's long-time best friend, and therefore like a surrogate sister. She spent a lot of time at my house as a kid, being a pest, so now she's family. It took a while for me to be okay with her dating Ballistic.

Not that he's a bad guy or anything. He's not. It's more that those two are probably the horniest pair on the face of the Earth, and we all have to bear witness to their constant mauling. It's a little weird for me. Not that Violet and I are any better— especially with how exuberant she can be.

Later this summer we're planning a trip to the Chicago cottage, and I'm really hoping those two can rein in their *fuckitude*, as Violet calls it. I'm also hoping Violet can manage to tone down her enthusiasm just a little.

"Who's putting the ink on her?" Lance asks.

"Hayden's designing it."

"Where's she want it to go?" Miller asks.

Randy shrugs and checks his phone when it vibrates. "We're gonna talk about it when we go in to look at the sketches. I'm kinda partial to her hip, but I think Lily might want it in a more visible spot, so we'll see."

"Hip tattoos are sexy on the ladies," Lance says, then frowns. "But doesn't that mean the artist will be all up in your girl's shit?"

"Huh?" Randy's still focused on his phone, which isn't unusual. He's often checking messages from Lily.

Lance points to his crotch. "He'll have his hands near her pussy, aye?"

"He'll be putting a tattoo on, not trying to finger-bang her," Randy snaps, but he starts stroking his beard, which means he's considering what Lance has accurately pointed out. "Besides, I'll be there with her the entire time."

"To supervise?" Lance needles.

"If you want to take this outside, let me know."

Lance grins. "Don't get yer panties in a twist, Balls. I'm just stating the obvious."

"Hayden's a professional. And she's not getting it until after the summer is over, so we've got lots of time to compromise on a location."

"We all carpooling? I can pick you up on the way." I nod to Darren, who's been relatively quiet. There's a ballgame on, though, and Darren likes to watch any sport, not just hockey.

"That works for me, but Charlene wants to come with."

"Is she thinking about getting ink?" Randy asks.

Darren shrugs. "Not that I'm aware. She's more of a steel girl."

"She's got a belly ring, right?" Randy asks.

"Sunny says she has her nipples pierced." Miller rubs his chest. "I get the belly ring, but I can't imagine it feels all that good when someone jabs a needle through your boob."

"According to Charlene, it's worth the pain, and it's sexy as fuck," Darren says quietly.

"So if she's already got her nipples and her belly done, what's left?" Miller asks.

Darren's grin isn't one I've seen before. "There are other, equally rewarding locations for steel."

Lance slaps the table. "Fuck, man! There was this bunny two seasons ago, before I was traded to Chicago, who had everything pierced, and I mean *everything*. It was insane. She was a little freaky. Wanted her friend to stick her whole arm up there."

"Sometimes I'm honestly baffled that you're ordained and able to marry people, when this is the stuff that comes out of your mouth. Is Water's and Violet's wedding even legit?" Randy asks.

Lance rolls his beer between his palms and stares at his glass.

"Just 'cause I've fucked a lot doesn't make it any less legit."

"Vi and I appreciate you doing that for us. The ceremony I mean, not the fucking." I clap him on the shoulder, and he flinches like I've surprised him. "Violet said she wants to come, too, so maybe Darren and I can carpool with the girls and meet you guys there?"

"Lily's coming along, since we're looking at her art at the same time."

"Sunny also wants to come," Miller says.

"I thought this was gonna be a team thing," Lance grumbles.

"Just pick up a bunny, and you can bring her along for the ride. Maybe she'll get your name tattooed on her boob," Miller says.

Randy gives him the eye. "Don't even joke. There are plenty of girls who've done that."

"Remember that chick who showed up at one of my parties with your number front and center on her pussy?" Lance asks.

"I'm pretty sure that was coincidental," Randy mutters.

His number is sixty-nine, so it's not a stretch.

"I'm just sayin'. Anyway, doesn't anyone find it kinda weird that all the girls want to come to a tattoo shop, and Lily's the only one looking to get a tattoo?"

"Charlene wants to look at jewelry," Darren adds.

"I think Sunny wants to come because Lily's coming, and Violet probably wants to come because Charlene is coming," Miller offers.

I don't bother to mention to the rest of the guys that Violet's asked me about nipple piercings. I have my doubts she's serious anyway. Violet's not one to invite pain intentionally, and I'm not willing to sacrifice her boobs. I already love them just the way they are.

GIRLS ARE WHACKED

LANCE

I pick up Randy and Miller—and Sunny and Lily—on Sunday morning so we can check out the designs at Inked Armor. I'm kind of fucking annoyed. Not because I don't like Lily and Sunny. I do. They're great girls. Ladies. Women. Whatever. But this whole thing is supposed to be about us guys getting tattoos together to commemorate the fact that we're part of the same damn team. What it's not supposed to be is this big fucking couple thing. Because that makes me super aware that I don't fit.

And I'm not trying to be a bitchy chick about it. Everyone but me has a girl. I mean, granted, I have lots of girls I can call, and I'm sure any one of them would be more than happy to hang out with me and a bunch of my professional-hockey-playing friends for an afternoon while we check out tattoo designs at one of the top studios in the city…as long as afterwards there's a fuck guarantee.

Unfortunately, bunnies and girlfriends do not mix. As a general rule, bunnies aren't interested in deep conversation—

with anyone. And what they want from me sure isn't chitchatting for several hours while surrounded by my friends in well-defined relationships.

I've learned from past experiences that all conversation does is give someone leverage, and I don't need anyone holding my own shit over my head, or using it to control me.

Hanging out with my teammates and their girlfriends—or wife, in Violet's case—isn't something I'm typically unhappy about. It's just that current circumstances are making me testier than usual. My ex—if I can even call her that since she never really acknowledged that it was a thing beyond fucking—has started texting me again, and I'm having a hard time not responding, despite the fact that I've changed her name from Tash to DO NOT FUCKING REPLY in my contact list.

My phone keeps buzzing in the center console.

Randy picks it up, checking to see who it's from, and frowns. "Is that who I think it is?"

"Yeah."

"What the hell does she want?"

"To fuck with my head some more? Who knows," I mutter.

Lily peeks her head over Randy's seat to get a look and sighs. "I would kick her in the vagina with my skates on for you."

"She'll stop messaging eventually." When I respond. Which could be a day, a week, or a month from now, depending on how long it takes me to cave. Then I'll get to spend an indeterminate amount of time afterwards feeling stupid for answering in the first place.

I put my phone to airplane mode so I don't get notifications every time she sends another message. It's still pretty early in the day, so parking isn't too hard to find close to Inked Armor. It's not my first time getting inked, but I like that I have a group of friends to do this with now, and that this piece will be a lot different than my other art.

Alex, Darren, Charlene, and Violet are all waiting for us down the street from the shop. Violet gives my arm a squeeze—it's as close as she usually gets to a hug. Ever since Alex had that on-ice accident last season, and I beat the shit out of the guy responsible, Vi and I have had a new appreciation for each other.

She appreciates my penchant for retribution, and I appreciate the strength of character it takes to go through shit like that with someone and decide they're worth the effort to stick it out.

I've seen more than one other teammate take that kind of hit and have their girlfriend, or fiancée, and even a wife or two decide they can't handle the pressure. Violet might be a little crazy, but she's got Alex's back when it matters. She's also a closet math nerd, like me.

Violet falls into step beside me. "Sorry we're crashing your sausage party."

"You're not crashing it."

"Yeah, we totally are. Mostly I'm here to observe and appreciate the fine art of tattooing."

"I didn't know you were into tattoos."

"Well, it's kind of erotic, right? Alex'll have to take his shirt off and this incredibly built guy covered in tattoos is going to get all up in his space and put something permanent on his skin." She fans her face. "So hot."

I shake my head, because that's not at all what getting a tattoo is like from my perspective, and only Violet could turn something that's supposed to be cool into something pornographic. "Except he's not actually getting a tattoo today," I point out. "Does Waters know you're here to ogle other guys?"

"Of course not! He thinks I'm considering getting my nipples pierced. And it's appreciating, not ogling."

"Jesus, Vi. You can't talk to me about your nipples. It breaks bro code."

She bumps my arm. "I'm not actually going to get it done."

"Still. I don't need to know anything about the state of your nipples."

"What the fuck are you two talking about?" Miller throws an arm around Violet's shoulder and grabs me by the back of the neck.

I elbow him in the ribs, and he lets go right away, but I'm betting he overheard our conversation, or at least Violet's side of the conversation, and that was his way of letting me know. There are conversations you should never have with your friends' wives and girlfriends; nipple discussions make that list.

"I was just telling Lance how I'm looking forward to seeing Alex get his nipples pierced."

Alex's head swings around. "Pardon fucking me?"

"Just kidding, baby. Your little man nipples are perfect the way they are, but if you want to get one of those peen piercings, I might be okay with it."

"Baby, you can barely handle me as is. What the hell do I need a piercing for?"

"I've been handling all you have to offer for more than a year. I'm pretty sure I can take a little steel ball.

"Okay. This is a conversation I expect to hear from Randy and Lily, not the two of you," Charlene says.

"Uh, yeah, there's no fucking way I'm putting extra holes in my junk, thank you very much," Randy says.

"It has its benefits," Darren replies.

Everyone turns to look at him.

"Seriously, what the hell do you two do in the bedroom?" Lily asks. "Never mind. I don't actually want to know."

Charlene fingers the pearls around her neck and looks up at Darren, who winks.

I'm relieved when we reach the storefront. The chick with the purple hair—I can't remember her name—comes out from behind the desk, throws the lock, and opens the door. "Hey! Hi! Oh, wow! It looks like everyone's here!"

"Hey, Lisa. Lily's coming to see what Hayden put together for her, and the rest of the girls wanted to tag along." Randy motions to them, standing in a gaggle behind him like they're his entourage, which wasn't far from reality not that long ago. Although it wasn't these girls falling all over themselves for him.

"That's great! Hey, guys! Hi, Violet!" She ushers us into the shop and locks the door. When we were all here for the initial consult, they had to move us to the private room so we wouldn't create a huge distraction.

There's another chick I've never met before seated behind the jewelry counter. She has long, dark hair that's been braided and pulled over her shoulder. She's wearing a loose tank that shows off a little ink on her shoulders. Maybe she's a friend of Lisa's.

I get an elbow in the ribs from Balls. "Don't even think about flirting with her. That's Tenley, Hayden's girlfriend."

"Thanks for the warning." I look away before she catches me staring. I don't want to piss off one of the guys who's going to put ink on my skin.

Lisa and Violet hug each other, and there's a round of introductions when Hayden, Chris, and Jamie, our team of artists, greet us.

We settle into the couches and chairs surrounding the coffee table on the left side of the room, and the girls follow, apparently interested in our designs.

Hayden opens a folder and methodically lines up sketch after sketch. "So these are some of the designs we've come up with."

The basis for each tattoo is the same: it's a puck that looks like it's just hit the ice with a cool blue watercolor background, but there are subtle differences in each one, beyond the incorporation of our names and numbers. Darren's is darker than the rest and is black and white, apart from his number, which is red. Waters has CAPTAIN underneath his and crossed sticks over the puck since he already has a puck tattoo, which is what our designs are based on—he'll just be adding to his. The inky looking background on Miller's is a brighter blue, Randy's is full, vibrant color, and mine has a more intense, deep blue.

I'm completely amazed by how well these guys have managed to capture our personalities through the art. No wonder Randy won't let anyone else work on him. I also understand exactly why this place is by appointment only.

"These are amazing," Randy says.

His declaration is followed by a chorus of agreements. Hayden drops his head, a small smile pulling at the corner of his mouth. His knee bounces a couple of times before he picks up another folder.

"Thanks. It really was a combined effort. We've got other options, though, and of course we expect to do some tweaking between now and the session, so know this isn't the final product. We can adjust color, design elements, font, all that stuff. You just have to let us know what's working and what isn't."

Flipping the folder open, Hayden pulls out a second set of designs with small, but significant differences. It doesn't take long for the girls to get bored with the back and forth over details. They head over to the jewelry case, where Lisa and Tenley are sitting, glancing at us every once in a while and whispering.

After a few minutes the girls—and by girls I mean Violet—get louder. Giggling and some gasps and *Oh my Gods* follow.

"I say go for it!" Charlene has her arm around Lily's shoulder.

"You won't regret it."

Randy looks up from the design. His is much different, considering it's going to be part of a sleeve. "Won't regret what?"

"Lisa's trying to convince Lily to get her clit pierced!" Charlene explains.

"Permanent vagina bling!" Violet chimes in.

"Jesus Christ," I mutter. "This is not stuff I need to know about."

Chris, the tattoo artist who's big enough to pass for a hockey player, or a linebacker, snorts. "You wouldn't believe the shit we hear on a regular basis."

"I don't think I even want to imagine."

Randy gives Lily a full-body visual sweep. His eyebrow rises. "What's the healing time on that?"

"That depends." Hayden says.

"On what?" Randy's knee is going now, and he's having a hard time not looking at Lily like he wants to eat her.

"On your level of patience. Isn't that right, kitten?" Hayden glances at his girlfriend.

Her eyes go wide, and her mouth drops open. "Seriously, Hayden?"

"What?" He looks genuinely confused, even though we're all suddenly super interested in the sketches, not the conversation. Well, except for Randy.

"I think you're badass for getting a hole in your vagina penis," Violet says seriously.

Chris barks out a laugh. "You guys need to hang out here more."

Lisa rolls her eyes, but she's smiling. She's the one who answers Randy's question. "If you follow the aftercare instructions, it's usually about a week before you can resume normal activity."

"Normal being—" He gestures between him and Lily. She looks a little mortified, which is kind of funny, considering how those two will pretty much get their fuck on anywhere. They routinely disappear for half-hour increments when they think no one's paying attention to them.

"You have to be careful with too much friction, too soon, or you'll prolong the healing period," Tenley replies.

"What do mean, *prolong*? Like, how sensitive is it going to be?"

"You gotta take it easy for a couple of weeks," Hayden says, eyes still on Tenley.

"Like, once a day easy?" Randy asks.

"Uh…" Hayden pokes the corner of his mouth with his tongue. I'm not sure if it's some kind of signal or what. "Yeeaah, you'll have to go easier than that."

Randy looks horrified. "Oh, fuck that. No way, luscious. I'm not going down to less than once a day."

"It has some incredible benefits." Tenley strokes her braid. She and Hayden are giving each other the screw-me eyes.

"What kind of benefits?" Randy still looks skeptical.

"More orgasms for Lily," Tenley replies.

Randy snorts. "Yeah, cause there's a real shortage of those right now."

"You probably couldn't get the needle through anyway since Lily's beaver is made of titanium," Violet says.

"Jealous again?" Lily smirks.

"It has nothing to do with jealousy. I'm just stating facts. Clearly you have some sort of beaver superpowers with the amount of humping you and Horny Nut Sac do."

"She's always like this, isn't she?" Chris asks me.

"Most of the time, yeah. It's pretty entertaining."

He nods his agreement. "How's she do with interviews and

stuff? "

"Those are always scripted," Alex says.

"What about nipples? What's the healing time on those?" Violet asks Lisa.

"About two months before they stop being sensitive, but a good four to six before they're totally healed, sometimes longer."

Violet makes a face and holds her boobs, so I look away.

Alex points a finger at her. "Don't even think about it, Violet."

"Oh, don't you worry. I would never take away your favorite toys for that long."

Alex relaxes back into his chair.

Charlene slaps the counter. "I'm going to do it!"

"You already have your nipples pierced. They're not ears; you can't get them done a whole bunch of times like Tenley here." Violet motions to Tenley's ears, which are indeed pierced numerous times. A ladder of rings climbs the shell.

Now, I don't have an issue with piercings. I've been with plenty of girls who have holes in various parts of their bodies—what I didn't realize is how long it takes for something like that to heal fully.

"I'm not talking about my nipples; I mean a hood piercing," Charlene clarifies.

Lisa does a little jumpy-squeal thing. "Yay! You won't regret it!"

"You're okay with that?" Charlene looks to Darren.

Darren taps the arm of the chair. His smile is tight. "If it's what you want. Although, you may want to consider waiting until the season starts and I'm on an away series."

Charlene bites her lip and turns to Lisa and Tenley. "It's only a week, though, right?"

"For gentle use," Tenley says.

Charlene looks back and forth between the girls and Darren.

"You can handle that."

"It's not me who has to go without. There are plenty of ways for me to achieve the same ends; not so much for you."

"He makes a good point," Lily says.

"I think I need to sit down." It's the first time Sunny's involved herself in the conversation since the girls started in on the piercing talk.

All of a sudden the girls are flitting around, and Miller's out of his seat. Sunny's pretty freaking pregnant right now, and she's a bit of a delicate flower—not literally, she's a yoga instructor, so physically she can kick ass. But she's not a big fan of blood or anything related to pain, so I can imagine this conversation is a little much for her.

I'm actually relieved that she's inadvertently put an end to it. Charlene seems to have decided to put off the piercing for another day, perhaps when Sunny isn't at risk of passing out on us.

When Sunny's recovered, the girls decide to make a trip to the coffee shop and bookstore across the street, and we get back to going over what we're here for: tattoo designs.

There's been some debate as to where we all want the tattoo, but it's not like we need to have them in the same place. Alex already has the puck-stick combo on his bicep, Randy's thinking about the top of his forearm, because he wants it on display, and I'm thinking I'll go with the inside of mine. Darren and Miller are both considering chest tattoos.

As we sit here, shooting the shit, I recognize that these guys have become my family. And that's as good as it is bad, because at some point I'm going to get traded again—we all are—and then I'll have to start over with a new team.

This tattoo is a good way to remember to hold on to these ties.

9

LOCATION RELOCATION

RANDY

Lily and I move to the private room with Hayden after we finish going over the team tats. I'm pretty damn excited to get started on this new sleeve, even though the appointment is a couple of months out. We want to wait until closer to the end of the summer when time in the sun won't distort fresh color. For now, it's something to look forward to. And I'm just as excited about Lily getting ink of her own.

Hayden pulls out Lily's folder. "Ready to see some designs?"

Lily gives me a huge smile before flashing it at Hayden. "So ready."

He withdraws three sketches, placing them on the table in front of us.

"Oh my God!" Lily claps a palm over her mouth and drops it just as fast. "These are beautiful. I want them all!"

Hayden chuckles. "So you like them?"

"I love them!" Lily hugs my arm. "Do you love them? Aren't they gorgeous?"

"They are, but that's what Hayden does." He and I exchange a look. Seeing Lily get excited about her first tattoo makes me remember exactly what it was like when I started mine. Although, having gone in wanting a full sleeve, I'd committed myself to a lot more time and art right from the beginning.

"Are you drawn to one over the others?" Hayden asks.

"Oh, God." Lily does this little bouncy thing and runs her hands down her thighs, which are bare since she's in a dress. "I don't know. They're all so perfect for different reasons. Which one do you like, Randy?"

I shake my head. "Nuh-uh. It's your art. That decision is yours."

"You don't have to choose right now. You can take some time to think it over," Hayden says.

She taps her lips. "I kind of want to get one right now."

Hayden and I laugh again. Her enthusiasm is hard-on inspiring. Although I've been sporting a semi pretty much the entire time I've been here with all the piercing talk and Lily giving me her sex eyes.

"You haven't even decided where you want it," I remind her.

She presses her knees together and looks up at me, then whispers. "I thought we said inner thigh."

"If that's where you want it, but you don't have to hide it from everyone but me if you want to put it somewhere it can be on display."

"Why do there have to be so many choices?" Lily complains, but she's still grinning. "Why can't this be easier so I can have it now?"

"Why don't we go over all your prospective locations, and the variables that impact them, and see if that helps you make a decision?" Hayden suggests.

Lily expels a breath. "Okay. Sounds good."

"So there are a few important things to consider once you've chosen the design. Placement is one of them, but so is the size of the tattoo. You can go bigger than this." He taps beside the design in the middle, then moves his finger to the one on the right. "But you can't go smaller than this unless we make some modifications. Otherwise we'll lose a lot of the detail, and the colors can bleed."

"Right, okay."

"If you decide you want the tattoo on your inner thigh, would you want it to be pretty small?" he asks, glancing between me and Lily.

She chews on her lip for a second. "I guess? Otherwise it would look kind of strange, right?"

Hayden taps the table. "Well, isolated, it might. If it was part of a series of tattoos, maybe not. But we want to treat this as the only one for now, right?"

"Good point."

"The other thing you might want to consider is that you'll likely have to be in your underwear for a couple of hours, and the inner thigh is sensitive for obvious reasons." Hayden's gaze stays fixed on Lily.

"I hadn't thought about that."

I sure have, ever since that conversation with Lance last week about the artist being up in Lily's business.

Hayden nods. "If you decide to get it on your hip, or that area, I'd say you might want to go this size—" He points to the smallest one. "—and depending on how low you're going, sometimes you're looking at towel coverage."

"Towel coverage?"

"He means no panties while he's putting it on." I try really hard to keep my voice even.

Lily's hand flutters to her neck. "Oh."

"Obviously we'd do it in here. And you'd have privacy when you change—"

"And I'm gonna be here," I bark.

Lily jumps a little, maybe at my tone.

"Sorry." I mutter.

Hayden gives me a knowing look. "You don't have to go with the hip if you don't want. You could put it on the back of your shoulder, or high up on your arm. Depending on how visible you want it to be, you could always get it on the inside of your forearm, or your ankle. I'd say the top of your foot, but with you being a figure skater, that's not a great place unless you have a couple weeks off to give it time to heal."

Lily traces the design in the middle. It's the one she keeps looking at the most. "I might need to think about the placement a little more."

"Once you settle on a design, I can make up a few transfers so you can see what it would look like in different locations. Then you can decide what you like best."

"Really?"

"Yeah. Of course. And I'll make copies of the designs for you to take with you. When you think you know which one you want, let me know, and if there are any changes, you can email them to me. Then we can schedule an appointment to check out placement. I can either book you on the same day the guys are coming to get their ink, or we can pick a different day."

Lily nods. "That sounds like a good idea."

Lily waits until Hayden leaves to make copies for her before she gives me the look I've been waiting for. This time it's nothing close to sex eyes.

"I know, I know. I'm sorry. I'm just not keen on the idea of some other guy's hands and face right up next to my favorite place to have my hands and face."

She puts her palm on my thigh. "And moody dick, don't forget him."

"Yeah. He's pretty unforgettable."

"I don't have to get it on my inner thigh."

"You can if that's what you want." It would be sexy, and I'll have to get over my serious aversion to Hayden's hands being that close to my girl's pussy if it's the location Lily decides to go with.

"Maybe it should be more visible."

"That might be nice, too." I'm way more partial to it being on her shoulder, or even her forearm, although I don't want it to interfere with her employability. It's irrelevant for me. Tattoos have no impact on my hockey career, but a highly visible tattoo on Lily might be different. It's another thing to discuss.

Hayden comes back a minute later with a rigid envelope that he passes over to Lily. "Usually I put them up in a place I like to hang out, like my living room or something, when I'm trying to make a decision."

"That's great. Thanks."

"Just call when you're ready, and we'll set up a follow-up appointment. Unless you want to do that now? Say, in a few weeks? I'm guessing you want to wait until summer's over since you've got a lot of light colors in there and you don't want the sun to fade them out."

Lily nods again, and we make an appointment for a few weeks from now, as well as another one for October, when I'll be home between a series of away games.

We finish up, and Lily hugs the envelope to her chest as Hayden opens the door to the private room and stops dead.

"What's going on here?" he demands. "You giving away all my treats while I'm busy?"

Everyone's sitting around eating snacks. It takes me a second to realize they're mowing down cupcakes.

Tenley, who's close to the same height as Lily, but curvier, flips her hair over her shoulder and gives Hayden a look I'm very familiar with. "Relax, *cupcake*, I made lots, and there are plenty at home if you don't get your fill here."

"Oh, I'm pretty sure I'll still be hungry when I get home, *kitten*."

Lily leans in to whisper in my ear. "And I'm pretty sure he's not going to be eating cupcakes."

"Neither will I," I whisper back.

10

CUPCAKE

TENLEY

I seriously can't get over the uncanny resemblance between Hayden and Randy. I mean, of course the beard is different, and Randy is way broader than Hayden, but put those two side by side, and they could probably pass for cousins, maybe even brothers.

Hayden has that look on his face—the one that tells me I'm the cupcake when I get home. Lily's whispering something to Randy, and ironically, he seems to be wearing a similar expression to Hayden's, and it's directed at Lily.

Suddenly the only place I want to be is home. In bed. With Hayden. If we can make it that far.

Lily excuses herself to the bathroom, and Randy watches her go.

"Stay where we can see you, Balls," Lance says.

"Those two like to christen bathrooms, and based on the look on this one's face, he's strongly considering following her." Violet points a finger at Randy.

"They have a lot in common with those two." Lisa motions between Tenley and Hayden.

"Like you're one to talk," Hayden shoots back.

"Jamie and I were never as bad as you two."

Hayden scratches his temple with his middle finger. "I think you have a short and faulty memory."

"You're riding shotgun on the way home." Lance points to Randy. "There's no way you and Lily are sitting beside each other."

There's some more banter back and forth, and when Lily returns they say their good-byes. I get Randy to sign the shirt and poster I brought to the shop before they leave. Everyone else is nice enough to sign it, too.

Lisa turns to me and fans herself once the door closes behind them. "That was a lot of testosterone."

"Right?"

"Can you even imagine what it would be like to date one of those guys? Their stamina must be insane."

Jamie stops filing designs in folders and gives Lisa a put-out look. "Uh, my stamina's insane."

"So is mine," Hayden says darkly.

Lisa gives Jamie a patronizing smile. "I didn't say it wasn't. All I'm saying is that these guys play professional sports for a living. Their job is to be physically fit."

Hayden runs his hand over his stomach. "I'm physically fit, aren't I, kitten?"

"Of course you are." For a guy who spends most of his time sitting in a chair, putting art on people's bodies, Hayden is incredibly fit. He runs, and we have a workout room in the house, so that helps.

"See?" Hayden flashes Lisa a dirty look. "I'm just gonna clean up a little in the private room, and then we can head home."

"I can help, if you want."

"You don't have to." He pauses at the door. "Unless you want to."

Chris is busy setting up for an appointment, and so is Jamie. Hayden is taking a rare Sunday afternoon off, so the sooner we leave, the sooner we'll get home and the sooner we can enjoy some naked time between the sheets, or on top of them.

I follow him into the private room, closing the door. I don't bother locking it. I'd prefer to be in a much more private location when he gets me naked.

"How was the consultation with Lily?" I ask, tracing the edge of the desk as I look over the designs he's sketched for her.

They're stunning, although everything Hayden creates is beautiful in my eyes, even if it's dark. These designs are anything but. A watercolor heart frames a pair of mismatched skates—one hockey skate and one figure skate tied together, the laces creating a second heart inside the first.

"Yeah. It went well." He taps the desk.

"That sounds like it comes with a but." I look up to see a little smirk curling the right corner of his mouth.

"She's really excited about the art, which is great—like, she would've gotten it today if she could've decided on a design."

"That's fantastic. So what's the problem?"

"Location." He drops down in his chair and wheels around the desk so he's beside me.

"You mean deciding whether she's wants it to be visible or not?"

"Yeah. Kinda. At first she mentioned inner thigh, and then I started explaining the logistics of that, so…"

I suddenly understand exactly what he's getting at. "Let me guess, Randy wasn't all that excited about you having your head between her thighs for a couple of hours."

Hayden shifts, grabs me by the hips, and pulls me between his legs. "You should've seen the look on his face when he realized what I was getting at. It was fucking priceless."

"Well, can you blame him? A sex god like you with your hands all over his girl?"

Hayden snorts. "I'm hardly a sex god, and those two seem pretty into each other."

"You're *my* sex god, and yeah, they're like a fuck-bomb ready to explode."

"I'm looking forward to being your fuck-bomb when we get home." Hayden slides his hands up the outside of my thighs until his fingers reach the waistband of my leggings. He slips his thumbs under and pulls it down far enough that I question whether he actually intends to make it home.

Hayden sweeps his fingers over the cupcake tattoo on the crest of my pelvis and follows with a soft brush of his lips. It was the first tattoo he ever put on me, a cover-up for a poorly done one I'd gotten as a teenager.

"Do you have any idea how much it pissed me off that someone inked you before me?"

I push his hair away from his eyes. "You were very clear about your feelings on that."

"I don't think I tried very hard to contain those." He's not even the least bit remorseful.

I laugh. "This is Lily's first tattoo, isn't it?"

"Yeah. It's cool to watch someone get excited like that, you know? I have a feeling it won't be her last, either."

I remember when Hayden put the cupcake on me. Beyond the intimacy, it was a huge rush. I'd never really counted the heart tattoo, so the cupcake felt more like a first. "I think you should design another tattoo for me."

"Do you now?"

"Mmm-hmm. It's been a while since I've been in your chair. I miss that feeling."

"You tell me what you want, and I'll draw it." Hayden's arms come around me and he looks up, his smile holding the same excitement as mine.

"I have some doodles at home."

Hayden stands. "Well, we should go there so I can check them. Then we can get you naked and decide where we want to put it."

"Best idea ever."

11

PAINT BY NUMBER

LILY

"This is so pretty. Isn't this pretty?" Sunny says for the fifth time on the ride home.

"It really is," Miller nods his agreement again.

"Can I have a look?" Lance asks when we're stopped at a red light.

I pass the photocopied sheet to the front for him to see.

He doesn't look at it long before he passes it back. "Nice."

I stare at it for a little while longer, still unsure which one I like the best. I wish Randy would state an opinion to help.

"So, the black skate is Balls here?" Lance thumbs over at Randy, who's sitting in the front seat beside him since he's not allowed to sit beside me. Again. It's smart. He's liable to get handsy, even if he says he won't.

"Uh-huh."

"Remember when that chick tattooed your name on her boob? Oh! Or the one who got your face, but it looked more like Jesus? Or that guy in that biker show?" Lance asks.

"Uh, yeah, that's not really a great comparison to Lily's tattoo." Randy shifts around uncomfortably.

"Right. Yeah." Lance must realize his mistake, because he doesn't say anything else.

He drops Sunny and Miller off first, because they live the closest, and then he drops Randy and me at our place.

As we get out, he checks his phone, rolls his eyes, and tosses it on the passenger seat beside him.

Randy eyes the device and then Lance. "You wanna come in and hang out for a bit?"

"Nah. I got some stuff to take care of this afternoon."

"We'll be around, if you change your mind," I say.

"Thanks." He smiles, but he looks sad as he waves and pulls away from the curb.

I slip an arm around Randy's waist. "I wish I had a friend to set him up with."

"That's a nice gesture, but probably not the best idea."

"Why not? Everyone deserves someone."

"Yeah, he's not really a one-someone kinda guy."

"He still seems pretty hung up on Tash for a guy who's not a one-someone kinda guy?" She was their old trainer.

"That situation was messy. It still is." Randy laces his fingers through mine.

"Our relationship was kind of messy when we first started hooking up."

We began as a casual fling, but clearly it didn't stay that way since I live with him now.

Randy regards me thoughtfully; then an evil grin spreads across his face. "You mean messy as in messing up the sheets? Or maybe you mean all the beard conditioning I had to do every time we hooked up?"

My mouth drops open, and I try to yank my hand away, intent

on tweaking his nipple, but he's wise, and a lot stronger than I am, so it doesn't work. He laughs and half-drags me up the front steps.

"You know I'm just playing, right?" He pulls me to him. I give him my cheek, so he kisses his way up my neck. "Well, not about the beard-conditioning part."

"You're winning no prizes with this."

"What if I tell you I want to condition my beard right now?"

"I'm all for public displays of affection, but I'm pretty sure we could get arrested for that, even if we're on our own front porch."

Randy fumbles with the keypad, punching in the code while he bites along my shoulder, his beard tickling me.

We manage to get inside the front door. I'm smart enough to set the envelope with the tattoo designs on the side table in the front hall before he gets me totally naked and makes good on his beard-conditioning promise.

It took me three days to decide on my favorite design. Randy never did voice any kind of opinion on it, but I saw him staring at the designs just as much as I was. Once I chose—I went for the biggest one with the most detail—we stopped by to see Hayden, and he sent me home with transfers. I've been wearing them all over my body for the past few days to help make a final decision on the location.

In this case, despite Randy's insistence that I be the one to make the choice, he's willing to help with the process. Using body paint.

"I thought you said this was out," I murmur as he nudges

my knees apart and dips his finger into the pink body paint. He draws a little heart high up on the inside of my thigh.

"I'm just making sure I don't want it here." Randy is not an artist by any stretch of the imagination. He is, however, very good at cleaning flavored paint off my body with his tongue. He's also very thorough. My preferred licking locations are obviously those close to the Vagina Emporium, which is right where he is now.

Of course, he doesn't stay there long, because he's a tease. He moves up until he can rest his chin on my pelvis—I'm only wearing panties and a camisole, so he has nearly full access to my currently unmarked skin. Using the purple paint, which tastes a lot like grape Kool-Aid, he draws a little smiley face on my hip.

"I really think when you retire from hockey, you should see if you can switch gears and apprentice with Hayden," I tell him.

"So you can start a fan club?" Randy covers the purple smiley face with his mouth and sucks the paint off, following up with a little teeth. I know he's kidding, though he's aware of all the girls' fascination with Hayden.

"Just imagine the fun places I'd be able to get tattoos if you were the one to put them on me."

I can't imagine we would ever finish one, to be honest.

He turns serious, even with his head between my legs. "You know you can have one wherever you want it."

I smile and run my fingers through his hair. It's getting long, which I love. "I know."

"I don't want your decision to be based on my insecurity." He kisses below my navel.

While an inner thigh or a hip tattoo would definitely be sexy, I'm not interested in slowing our sex roll with new ink. Even if I waited for him to be on a series of away games, he'd still have to be gentle for at least a week. Sometimes Randy and I have slow, sweet sex. But that's the exception, definitely not the rule.

Beyond that, I want the tattoo to be visible—not necessarily all the time, but at least during the summer months. "I still think my shoulder is the perfect location. That way it's visible when I want it to be and easily covered when I don't."

Also, Randy likes to kiss me there, so now he'll have an actual target. It's a special, meaningful tattoo, tied to so many good memories.

"Wherever you get it, it's gonna be sexy." Randy pulls himself up higher, kissing his way across my stomach.

"Well, I doubt it's going to be my last one, so there's plenty of opportunity to find other places, isn't there?"

"Fucking right." Randy settles between my thighs.

I circle my arms around his neck. I toyed with putting the tattoo on my forearm, but I don't know if I'm ready for that level of visibility quite yet. I need to ease my poor mother in to this, one pretty design at a time.

In the meantime, I get to experience the excitement that comes with planning out a new sleeve with Randy. As I run my hands up his arms, one marked, one waiting to be marked, I understand his love of body art in a way I never did before.

It's about wearing a piece of your history, a part of what makes you who you are. And sometimes it's about the people who come into your life, and embed themselves in your heart until you can't imagine where you'd be without them.

Read on for a preview of Fractures in Ink

FRACTURES

in Ink

PROLOGUE

CHRIS

Hot, wet suction and a discordant chilly tickle across my stomach pulled me from sleep. It took a few seconds to figure out what was going on.

"Sorry I woke you."

Sarah, who I'd been seeing for the past six months, followed her insincere statement with the return of her mouth to my very awake cock.

The rest of me took a little longer to shake off the haze.

"Time is it?" I reached out in the dark to touch some part of her. I met damp hair. She must've come directly from the shower.

"Late." She licked up the shaft, making me groan.

The clock on the nightstand told me it was three a.m., in glowing red numbers. Sarah's late arrival wasn't unusual. She worked long hours as a waitress at a strip club just outside the Chicago Loop. Middle-of-the-night visits were sometimes all we could manage. "Don't you have an early class?"

She popped off, but her lips moved against the head as she spoke. "You're worried about what time my class is right now?"

I hooked my hands under her arms and pulled her up, then

flipped her over.

"I wasn't done," she complained.

"I think that's my new favorite alarm clock."

Sarah parted her legs so I could fit myself between them. She was so, so naked. I kissed along her neck; her skin was shower-warm and damp. She'd used my body wash, but her hair smelled like the shampoo she kept in my apartment for nights like these—mint and rosemary.

Sarah linked her legs behind my back and smoothed her hands down my arms, over the ink she couldn't see in the dark. She made an impatient noise when I brushed my lips over hers but ignored her invitation for tongue.

"Kiss me." She nipped at my bottom lip.

"You don't want me to rinse with mouthwash? I think I have mints in the nightstand."

She gripped the back of my neck, her fingernails digging in as she fused her mouth to mine. I guess she didn't care about sleep breath.

Sarah was rarely aggressive when it came to sex. She liked things soft and easy most of the time, and she got off on the teasing almost as much as the actual fucking. But not tonight—or this morning, as it were.

She shifted against me, lining everything up. I was still half foggy from being woken by a blow job.

I pulled back, which wasn't easy with the way she was latched on to my neck and my tongue. "Take it easy, sugar."

"I missed you." Her fingers danced across my cheek. "I want you."

"You got me. I'm right here."

Sarah couldn't seem to decide what she wanted to do with her hands. They were in my hair, down my back, grabbing my ass as she lifted her hips and I slid low. She was ready with the condom before I could protest again and slow us down.

I stopped fighting what she wanted. It'd been a week since we'd seen each other. If she didn't have to leave too early in the morning, we could have a slower second round.

When she pushed on my chest, I rolled to the side and lay down beside her. Sarah's wet hair swept across my neck as she straddled my hips. It was too dark to see the soft, delicate features of her face as she rolled on the condom and took me inside. She braced her palms on my chest as she rode me, swiveling her hips, grinding hard until she came. She was nearly silent, emitting only the faintest moans, barely audible over the sound of the fan running in the corner of my room. I knew she was coming only by the way her rhythm faltered and her nails dug into my skin.

Once she had what she needed, she let me take over. I moved her onto her back, rolling my hips without urgency. My eyes had adjusted to the lack of light. The blackout shades kept the glow of the streetlights outside and residents of the neighboring apartment building from seeing things they shouldn't.

"Give me your mouth, baby," I murmured in her ear.

Her nose brushed across my cheek, lips following the same trail until I caught her mouth with mine again. I stroked against her tongue and she arched, arms and legs wrapped tightly around me again. I followed the long, toned line of her left thigh until I reached her knee. Pulling it higher, I tucked her leg against my ribs so I could go deeper without changing the tempo.

"Chris." Sarah's whimper was followed by a shudder. Her fingertips dragged soft down the side of my face, close to our touching lips.

"You coming again?"

She nodded and pressed her face into my neck, her soft moan muffled by my skin. It didn't take me long to come after that.

Afterward, Sarah snuggled into my side and stayed there, which was also unusual. Typically I'd get a couple minutes of closeness out of her, and then she'd complain about being hot and move away. But not tonight. She kept her head on my chest and traced the lines of my sleeve until I fell asleep.

I woke a few hours later to the feel of fingers tickling my arm. I turned to find Sarah lying on her side, her pale blond hair fanned out across the pillow. She snatched her hand away and pressed her knuckles to her mouth. Her sea blue eyes were red rimmed, like she needed more sleep. She closed them and inched closer, her whole body pressing against me before her lips connected with the ink on my shoulder.

I pushed unruly blond away from her forehead, then traced the heart shape of her face. Sarah nuzzled her cheek against my arm for a few seconds, a shuddery sigh warming my skin.

"You got time for some morning lovin'?" I rasped, my voice less awake than the rest of me, just like it had been last night, or much earlier this morning.

"I need the bathroom." She rolled away and threw off the covers. The room was still mostly dark, but I could make out her willowy silhouette as she tiptoed across the room, naked, and slipped out the bedroom door.

I checked the time. It was only seven. She had to be exhausted, but I assumed her going to the bathroom meant morning sex was on the menu. Priorities and all.

Except when she returned ten minutes later, she was fully dressed. Her white blouse was crisp and buttoned almost to her throat. She'd pulled her long hair up into a bun, the style too severe for her pretty face.

I folded an arm behind my head. "Not getting back into bed with me?"

She traced the edge of the footboard, her head bowed. "I can't. I have class."

"Wanna come give me a kiss goodbye?"

Her voice was a whisper I had to strain to hear. "I think we need to take a break."

I hit the light on the nightstand so I could see her better. "What kinda break you talking about?"

"My internship starts soon. I'll be working a lot of hours. At both jobs. I'm exhausted, and I think something's got to give." Her voice wavered, as if she were on the verge of tears.

The conversation wasn't unexpected. Of course I'd be the something she was ready to give up. I'd known this day was coming, eventually, since the moment she'd agreed to go out with me. Still, I stared at her for a few long seconds, trying to see the motivation that pushed her to this decision now.

Maybe she'd finally realized she was too good for me—that she was out of my league and could find someone better, someone who could give her the things I couldn't. Sarah deserved a nice life with a pretty house and a fancy car she didn't have to worry about. I wasn't that guy.

For her, it seemed I was mostly a middle-of-the-night booty call, which was ironic because for years I'd been the one to pull that move. I guess it was about time I experienced it from the other side.

"You want to call it quits?" I asked.

She lifted one slight shoulder, still tracing imaginary lines on the footboard.

"So last night was the goodbye fuck and the see-you-later blow job?" That would definitely explain the aggression.

"We barely see each other." She swiped at her eye with her

pinkie before she lifted her head, but her gaze didn't quite meet mine. "It's not going to get better once I start my internship."

As much as I didn't want to admit it, she had a point. We'd been treading water for months now; it was only a matter of time before we sank. "You're right. It probably won't."

"I'm sorry, Chris. I need to stay focused on school. Maybe after it's over, when things settle down again..."

"Yeah. I don't know about that." I had my doubts that Sarah would want to keep doing this with me once she'd had a break. One of the guys in her program would jump all over her being single, and she'd see me for the mistake I'd been all along. Sarah and I weren't meant to be permanent, and this was exactly the reminder I needed. "You gotta do you, sugar."

She bowed her head, fingers fluttering up to cover her eyes. Her back expanded in a deep inhale. On the exhale she dropped her hands and squared her shoulders, but her next statement still came out a question. "I'll leave your key on the counter."

"Sure. If that's what you want to do."

She gave one final nod before she left.

The emptiness was a lot bigger than I'd expected it to be.

ONE

CHRIS

Two weeks later

Inked Armor was humming today, and not just with the sound of tattoo machines. Waiting clients sat in the chairs by the windows, leafing through ink magazines and chatting with the person they'd brought along for the ride. College girls colluded at the body jewelry case, deciding what kind of piercing would have the most benefits.

In the five years since we'd opened the shop, it had never been this busy. And ultimately that was a good thing, though my business partner, Hayden Stryker, probably joined me in wishing it was strictly due to our mind-blowing skills and artistry. Instead, a few months back we'd gleaned quite a bit of unintentional media attention.

Hayden had been seventeen when his parents were murdered. He'd been the one to find them shot in their own bedroom when he came home three hours after curfew. But he'd never known why they were killed, or who killed them. Then after seven years, last winter Hayden had finally—and rather publicly—gotten the answers he was looking for.

The trial hadn't lasted long, thank Christ, but I was still trying to get my head around its aftermath.

I'd met Hayden not long before his parents died. Over the years he'd become my family, and his pain was mine. He'd been into piercings more than ink when we were first introduced, so I hadn't gotten to know him until Damen—the guy who ran Art Addicts, the shop where I'd worked at the time—took him on as an apprentice. While the shop had been legit, Damen had also had some criminal leanings, including a drugs-and-prostitution ring he ran at The Dollhouse, a local strip club. But we'd needed the opportunity and the steady pay, so we kept our heads down. But time had given us perspective we hadn't had then. My choices had been limited, and my focus had been on survival. Damen had taken me in when I had nowhere else to go.

Anyway, along with the horror of reliving it all and the sheer emotional overload of finally understanding what had happened, the trial and its media coverage had yielded Inked Armor a schedule booked solid with appointments made months in advance.

Recently, a local pro hockey player and some of his teammates had come in for tattoos, so it was even crazier that day. Not that I could complain. Much. Our paychecks were nicely padded, and Inked Armor had earned some serious recognition in the tattooing community. After all the shit we'd dealt with, it was good to have some positive outcomes.

The door tinkled with the arrival of a group of girls who headed straight for the jewelry counter. Lisa, the shop piercer and bookkeeper sometimes had to schedule the piercings a couple of days in advance depending on how busy we were.

My client, Eric, watched them swarm the jewelry case. "Does it ever slow down in here?"

"Not lately. You know how it is. We've been booked pretty

solid with summer coming." This time of year was always busy—people wanting to add art they could display during shorts and T-shirt weather—but this far surpassed that.

"Oh I get it. I would've been in here a month ago if I could've gotten an appointment."

"Lisa's already scheduled your next two sessions, so we just have to make sure the dates work for you."

"I'll make 'em work if I have to."

I'd overbooked today, leaving me no time between clients. When this session was over, the next one would take me to closing. The less free time I had these days, the better.

My phone buzzed in my pants, and my automatic response was to check the apartments across the street since my hands were busy with the needles.

From Inked Armor's front window I had a perfect view of the converted house across the street, which boasted a café and bookshop at street level and two apartments on the second floor. Sarah lived in the one on the right. I hadn't seen her up close since she'd left my apartment two weeks ago. Her exit from my bed and my life continued to leave a much bigger void than I'd expected.

Prior to fourteen mornings ago, a buzz in my pants had usually meant a message from Sarah. And often I'd see her silhouette in the window, especially if she was waiting for me to drop by when I had a break between clients.

As I looked there now, the curtain in her window fluttered with movement, though if it was Sarah, she clearly didn't want to be seen. That had been happening a lot lately—for the past two weeks, to be more specific. But the messages I'd sent her remained unanswered, so I had my doubts this latest text was her looking to talk, unless she'd changed her mind about me recently.

The apartment window to the left of hers remained dark, the blinds pulled shut. The space was currently unrented. Hayden's girlfriend, Tenley, used to live there, but she'd moved into his house. Hayden had hung up his bachelor balls shortly after he met her, and they'd settled into domesticated stability. They even had a cat, which he'd named after Tee. I made fun of him often, and he didn't give a shit.

I doubted Tee's old apartment would remain vacant for long, considering the prime location near DePaul University. Some student would take it over soon. I'd entertained moving there myself before me and Sarah went on the outs. It would be totally convenient for work. But now that would make things even more awkward. Besides, rent was cheap where I lived, and moving my shit would be a pain in the ass. At least those were the excuses I went with.

I turned back to the art I was outlining, pausing before I started a new line of ink. "You need a break or anything? Water?"

"Nah, I'm good to keep going."

In the four hours he'd been here I'd only stopped once. When the design was complete, it would span his entire back. Today we were finishing the basic outline and some of the minor detail. I loved working on the Celtic designs. The intricacy and the detail allowed me to get lost in the art for hours. Except not right now, because I couldn't seem to manage my divided attention, and that was because of Sarah.

I wasn't sure why this was such a big deal for me. I was used to not getting what I wanted. Over the years it had been a pretty common occurrence. Anything remotely good in my life was fairly fleeting, and Sarah was a master's student in a business program. Her tuition cost more than my yearly salary, based on the research I'd done. Her starting wage after she graduated would likely be double what I made in any given year, even one as good as this.

I'd met Sarah at The Dollhouse, back before it had been shut down. She'd only ever been a waitress there, never up on the stage or pulled into the darker side of the industry. But even serving drinks was no picnic since most of those assholes couldn't keep their hands or their comments to themselves. It was almost as bad as getting naked and swinging from a pole.

The Sanctuary—Sarah's current place of employment—boasted an elite staff and a classy vibe, but its polished veneer was just that: a false face. It might've seemed better than The Dollhouse, but I had a feeling underneath the clean exterior was a dark and dirty interior Sarah wasn't talking to me about.

And it hadn't ever been anything I'd pushed to hear. Encouraging her to talk about it had meant she might feel like asking me questions about my own history, and that wasn't a place I'd wanted to go with her. We'd kept things pretty light, our protective walls firmly in place, which was probably why we lasted as long as we did.

I'd always figured if there was a real issue, she'd say something. But maybe I'd been wrong about that, just like I'd been wrong about predicting the end of this thing we'd had going.

Anyway, Sarah's work wardrobe might currently consist of skimpy dresses, but she'd soon be trashing those for the kind of buttoned-up outfit she'd been wearing that morning two weeks ago. This was just another sign that Sarah and I were on different paths, moving in opposite directions. My uniform wasn't going to change; I'd still be wearing jeans and a T-shirt bearing the Inked Armor logo a few years from now.

I swiped at the ink with a damp cloth, wiping the site clean to make sure the lines were clear before I continued. "We're getting close. Another ten and you can check it out."

Eric rolled his neck. He had to be stiff from sitting in the same position for so long. "Looking forward to it."

I glanced briefly at the girls who had relocated to couches while they filled out body-piercing paperwork. They looked like college students. One of them gave me a flirty smile, which I returned before refocusing on the ink. I was glad I was too busy to be chatted up, considering where my mind was these days.

I hadn't been under any illusion that what Sarah and I had was going to turn serious. Except based on the way I was dealing with her exit, it kind of had anyway. At least on my end. I'd gotten used to her nearly daily messages. I'd enjoyed the mornings I woke up with her in my bed.

And I'd wondered what it would be like if that turned into *every* morning. Which was fucking stupid. Because deep down I knew I was a temporary fixture in her life. I was the second-hand sofa college students bought, trashed for a while, and later traded in for a nicer one.

Sarah was destined to upgrade.

The thing was, since she'd broken things off, she'd also stopped talking to some of our mutual friends. She and Lisa had been close, but Lisa said her texts and phone calls to Sarah had gone mostly unanswered over the past two weeks. I couldn't decide whether it was Sarah feeling weird about talking to Lisa since I worked with her, or more than that. My gut told me it was the latter.

The more I thought about it—obsessed, really—the more I questioned whether Sarah's reason for walking was honestly her internship, or if there had been something else going on. The way it went down hadn't sat right with me. The lack of warning was part of the problem. There'd been no awkward lead up, no signs things were about to take a shit, and I was usually pretty good at predicting when the bottom was going to fall out.

I dipped the needle into black ink and touched up a few lines. I hoped Sarah's silence would end eventually, particularly where Lisa was concerned. Just because we weren't middle-of-the-night fucking any more didn't mean she had to cut all ties with the people she'd gotten close to. And honestly, Lisa was just as concerned as I was about Sarah's sudden silence.

Lisa had once worked at The Dollhouse too, and her past experiences, combined with what had come out about the inner workings of those places during the recent trial, were good reason to worry.

I put the finishing touches on the outline and set down my tattoo machine. "All right, man, that's it. Wanna take a look?"

"Fucking right." He sat up stiffly, stretching his arms over his head. I followed him to the three-way mirror, my stomach tightening a little while I waited for his approval.

He clapped me on the shoulder. "This is unreal. Thanks, man."

Hayden came over to check it out while I was dressing the tattoo and reviewing aftercare. Then we checked the dates on Eric's next two sessions before he left happy, and probably sore.

I still had a few minutes before my next client, so I checked my messages. There were two. Neither was from Sarah.

These were from Candy, a chick I used to date long before Sarah and I started warming each other's beds. I doubted it was a coincidence that she'd started messaging me this week, wanting to get together for a drink.

It was pretty clear she had ulterior motives, so I'd put her off, saying I was busy, but her persistence was wearing me down—though not because I wanted, or needed, a hook up. I didn't. And especially not with her. Still, over the past few days, Candy's messages had grown progressively more insistent. Her most recent informed me that she had some information I might want.

It was hard not to wonder who or what it pertained to.

Things with Candy hadn't ended well. I'd met her while she was working at The Dollhouse, and she'd been in the same position as Sarah and Lisa—just serving drinks, not getting up on stage. But the slope was slippery, and Candy found the money to be a lot better when she was taking her clothes off and grinding on the pole.

Then she started hitting the back rooms after sets for private dances. It didn't take long to turn into fucking. Between that and the drugs I'd been working hard to stay away from, I couldn't deal, so I bailed.

Normally I wouldn't even entertain the idea of seeing her, for all of the previously mentioned reasons—but Candy now worked at The Sanctuary with Sarah. I could only guess what the information might be, and that was driving me crazy. Since I wasn't going to get anything out of Sarah directly, it might not hurt to go in through the back door.

Candy had been pissed when I started seeing Sarah, to the point that she'd made life miserable for her at the club—although Sarah had downplayed it, as she was prone to doing. I suspected that if I agreed to see Candy, she'd rub it in Sarah's face. It wasn't the nicest way to go about things, and I wasn't one to play games, but any reaction right now was better than no reaction at all. If I could piss Sarah off enough, maybe she'd talk to me. Shady and shitty, but I needed some answers, and I wanted to make sure she was okay.

I needed to keep tabs on her until she was out of that place for good. We might not be meant for the long haul, but I didn't want her pulled down into a lifestyle that could turn her into another Candy.

I stared at Candy's messages for a few more seconds before I hit her back. Once I did, my phone beeped right away, asking if tomorrow would work. Before I replied, I scrolled through my messages from Sarah. Or mostly my messages to Sarah, because the last one I'd gotten from her was the night before she broke it off, telling me how she couldn't wait to fight me for sheets.

I typed out a message to Candy and hit send. Her reply was the kind I used to like getting from Sarah, with all the heart and smiley face emoticons. I had a hard time believing Candy's was sincere, though.

Lisa's arm came around my shoulder, her lavender hair tickling my cheek. Lisa was small, narrow lines filled out by *Alice in Wonderland* dresses and combat boots. Her hair was always some pale rainbow shade. "Your next appointment's in fifteen. You need to set up."

She snatched my phone before I could shut it down and jumped out of reach when I grabbed for it.

"What're you doing?" I snapped.

"What am I doing? What're you doing?" She held up my phone, pointing to the contact. "We need to talk."

"I gotta set up."

Lisa dug her nails into my arm and pulled me out of my chair. I could've argued, but then I'd draw more attention our way. Hayden or Jamie—the other artist in the shop and Lisa's fiancé—might notice and want to know what was going on. Neither would approve of me spending time with Candy.

I followed her to the storage room. She pushed me inside and closed the door. "Seriously, Chris? *Candy?*"

"It's not what you think."

She crossed her arms over her chest. "So you're not going for coffee tomorrow morning. I read that wrong?" Lisa knew Candy only too well, having worked with her and been around us when Candy and I were dating.

"I'm trying to get information. Sarah won't talk to me."

"There are better ways to do that than through Candy."

"Really? 'Cause I'm all outta options right now."

"Just call her."

I slapped my own forehead. "Why didn't I think of that?"

Lisa gave me one of her looks.

"I've even left messages. She won't respond. The only thing I haven't done is go to her work, and that's not happening, 'cause I'm not real interested in revisiting my juvie days, and I have a feeling that's what's going down if I go there."

"And you think Candy's going to tell you what's going on? When Sarah finds out she's going to freak."

I moved the rolls of paper towels so they were lined up straight. Usually that was Hayden's habit, but I needed to do something with my hands.

"Enough that she'll talk to me?"

"That's your motivation? Push Sarah's buttons? That could backfire on you pretty bad."

"Candy says she has information I might want."

"Candy's a manipulative bitch."

"I know, but something's not right."

"You don't think Sarah's dancing, do you?"

"I don't fucking know. It's a logical conclusion, isn't it? One second she's all excited about a sleepover, comes over and rides me like I'm a goddamn theme park, and the next morning she tells me we can't see each other any more. Then she pretty much stops talking to all of us."

Lisa fiddled with the piercing above her lip. "I invited her to hang out with me and Tenley later this week."

"What? Why didn't you tell me?" Jesus. I hated how pissed off I sounded. "Wait. Let me guess; she didn't want me to know."

"Honestly, I called her last night and managed to get her on the phone. I seriously didn't think she was going to say yes, but she did. I'm crossing my fingers she doesn't bail." She put a hand on my forearm. "I won't hide things from you. If she shares something I think you need to know, I'll tell you, even if it's something you won't want to hear."

I tapped the space between my eyes. I was gonna have one hell of a headache by the end of the day. "If she's on the pole, it's a good thing she ended things, 'cause I'm not going down that road again."

"But you'll go out for coffee with Candy?"

"It's not the same. I'm only seeing her to get information." I changed the subject. My relationship with Candy wasn't a favorite topic, and I wanted details from Lisa. "What are you doing with Sarah?"

"We're getting together with Tenley. Girl's night kind of thing. It took a lot of persuading to get her to agree. She feels awkward."

"She said that?"

"Not in so many words."

"Right." It felt like a kick in the balls that Sarah would make time for Tee and Lisa, but when it came to quitting me, she'd delivered a one-paragraph monologue, and then cut out.

My phone buzzed again with another message from Candy. She wanted me to pick her up in the morning. I let her know I'd meet her there since I had a few errands to run. I knew how Candy worked. If I came to get her, she'd want me to come up to her apartment, and that would lead to situations I wasn't interested in entertaining.

I didn't think I was at risk of getting involved with her again, but sometimes the head on my shoulders didn't work all that well. I'd give myself all the help I could.

New York Times Bestselling Author
HELENA HUNTING

NYT and USA Today bestselling author of PUCKED, Helena Hunting lives on the outskirts of Toronto with her incredibly tolerant family and two moderately intolerant cats. She writes contemporary romance ranging from new adult angst to romantic sports comedy.

Find more books by Helena Hunting
by visiting helenahunting.com

CPSIA information can be obtained
at www.ICGtesting.com
Printed in the USA
LVOW03s1954260418
574991LV00013B/1174/P